GLADIATOR ISLAND

ISLAND

The War Design

COREY O'NEILL

E

EPIC
Press

The War Design
Gladiator Island: Book #5

Written by Corey O'Neill

Published by EPIC Press™
PO Box 398166
Minneapolis, MN 55439

Cover design by Laura Mitchell
Images for cover art obtained from iStockPhoto.com
Edited by Leah Jenness

LIBRARY OF CONGRESS CATALOGING-IN-PUBLICATION DATA

Names: O'Neill, Corey, author.
Title: The war design / by Corey O'Neill.
Description: Minneapolis, MN : EPIC Press, [2017] | Series: Gladiator Island ; book #5
Summary: As Reed and his friends consider revolting to escape the island, a traitor is sharing
    their plans with Gareth every step of the way. With the walls closing in on them, Reed and
    his allies must stay alive long enough to put their plan into motion.
Identifiers: LCCN 2015959401 | ISBN 9781680762716 (lib. bdg.) |
    ISBN 9781680762921 (ebook)
Subjects: LCSH: Adventure and adventurers—Fiction. | Interpersonal relationships—Fiction. |
    Survival—Fiction. | Human behavior—Fiction. | Young adult fiction.
Classification: DDC [Fic]—dc23
LC record available at http://lccn.loc.gov/2015959401

EPICPRESS.COM

For Vanessa

CHAPTER 1

Reed

I'd lost track of how many weeks we'd been on the island, but I felt like a different person entirely since when my parents had found me blacked-out drunk, passed out in my backyard. I was now sober for the first time in two years, and my mind was completely clear. The drugged out, numb Reed was gone.

Here on the island, I had no way to try to dull the pain of everything that filled my mind. And in the long stretches of time each night—after bedtime and before I slept—often all I could think about was murder. With every battle, killing my opponents got a little easier to stomach. And if I was being honest, each time was more satisfying than the last.

It felt almost good to kill Odin after he had tormented me, and now I fantasized about how I'd murder Gareth if given the chance.

I was frightened by how quickly my personality was changing. Although I could reason that everything I'd done was for the sake of survival, it felt like something violent had been awakened inside of me.

When I thought about my chances at survival, I knew I'd have to embrace that impulse when the revolt began—to fight for my life one last time.

Battling the Creature in the Coliseum was a rude awakening—and terrifying. And after Elise told Delphine and me about Gareth's kill switch—his ability to blow up the island if backed into a corner—I was worried. It meant we'd have to be extremely careful with the next stages of the plan.

I wondered what my dad would think once I got to talk to him—his son raised from the dead. Would he believe me and the crazy story I had to tell?

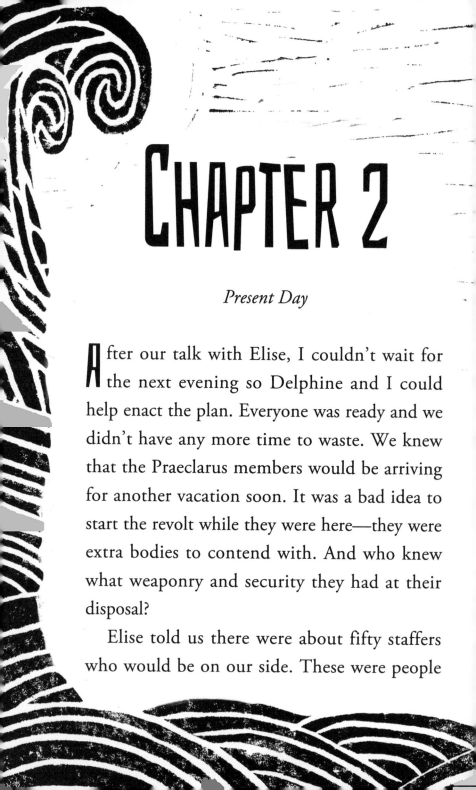

CHAPTER 2

After our talk with Elise, I couldn't wait for the next evening so Delphine and I could help enact the plan. Everyone was ready and we didn't have any more time to waste. We knew that the Praeclarus members would be arriving for another vacation soon. It was a bad idea to start the revolt while they were here—they were extra bodies to contend with. And who knew what weaponry and security they had at their disposal?

Elise told us there were about fifty staffers who would be on our side. These were people who would put up a fight once we had the means to get out of here safely. And they all relied on me reaching my dad, him finding us, and my dad aiding our escape before we were killed.

If fifty staffers were on our side, I estimated that meant there were at least one hundred who were not—about one hundred people living on the Island who still supported Gareth. We were definitely outnumbered. And even though the odds felt stacked against us, I knew there was no other choice. We'd all be killed sooner or later. We had to put up a fight and not let Gareth take us out easily.

With the right resources and a means to escape, I thought we had a shot to make it out alive. But we'd have to be sure Gareth wouldn't just blow up the whole island at once with his kill switch. Elise thought it wasn't likely, but how could she really know?

And something else was bothering me. I couldn't help but think about Chelsea and wonder

where she was being held. Gareth was punishing her for betraying him in the Coliseum in front of all of Praeclarus. I didn't believe that he'd try to save her when the fighting began.

I didn't want her to be locked up. What if everyone got killed or escaped, and Chelsea was trapped in a cell somewhere with no one able to help her? That thought made my stomach turn, picturing her rotting away with no way out as we were on a boat or helicopter leaving this place behind.

I imagined fighting a war to leave the island, one that would leave it in ruins. I couldn't just leave believing Chelsea was trapped somewhere against her will. Against my better judgment, I sympathized with her. She showed signs of being good, of being sorry for everything she'd done.

And then I thought about Delphine and that she had to spend the night with Gareth again. It was disgusting to me, the way he used girls young enough to be his daughters. When Delphine returned from those visits, she always seemed angry, but not broken. By now, I was certain she was tougher than all of us.

CHAPTER 3

After being woken up by Suits, we got dressed in our training gear. I put on my white shorts and tank top and looked over at everyone else as we headed to the dining hall. There were nearly thirty kids in total. I was sure they'd all want to escape and have the chance to live a normal life if they were presented with the opportunity.

Most of the kids hated me now, though, since I killed Odin. He'd been like a leader to them. But once they discovered that I could be their ticket to freedom, I was confident they'd change their tune about me and join me. We just had to enlist them at the right time, before

Gareth could have the chance to turn them to his side.

I was feeling very anxious for the evening to start already. Our plan would begin in earnest tonight—we'd be contacting my dad. And if everything worked, I'd finally get to talk to him and let him know I was alive, and that I was sorry, and that I needed his help to find us and to get us out.

Max led us out to the training area. Having spent hours every day there for months, it felt like I knew every inch of it too well—the grass that flattened underfoot, the dirt and rocky patches. The sun in the training area was unrelenting and cruel, with no shade except in the very corners, under the overhang, and next to the walls—small slivers of darkness that shifted across the space as the day progressed.

In that moment, I hoped it was one of the last days I'd ever stand there in the middle of the training floor.

This place was changing my view toward my

own mortality. I was restless and achy and discontent. The Island was making me feel less remorse with each person I killed. It was a necessity—what needed to be done to survive. I just blocked the person's face out of my mind, not seeing their cheeks and eye sockets crushed and bleeding, or the tangled and cut limbs, or the bloody stillness, just after death.

We started the morning routine of running the track, and I elbowed my way past everyone else as they grunted and pushed back at me, talking shit. We couldn't help but make it a game, jostling for first place and angling to prove who was strong and who was weak.

I always pushed myself to the front, determined to assert myself in every exercise we were given. I had to not show any signs of cracking, of letting this place get to me, of distraction, even if that was all true on the inside. I couldn't let on that the escape was just around the corner—not yet.

Today, as I came around the bend to the finish

line, Ames waved me over to meet him by the water fountain. I jogged to him and bent down to get some water. I looked back and the others were being wrangled by Max to begin our morning stretching. No one seemed to pay us much attention. We often talked together—everyone knew that Ames had taken a liking to me ever since my first day in the elite training area. They just didn't know why.

"You ready, my friend?"

He looked at me very sternly and I nodded.

"Everything's going to start tonight, but who knows where it might end. Are you sure you're up for this?"

"Of course," I said, fully aware that we might set something in motion that would lead to our deaths. I didn't see any choice in the matter, though. We had to fight back as a united front to even have a chance of escape. "I'm ready for whatever Gareth brings."

Then I hesitated, not sure if I should say what I was thinking.

"What is it?" he asked, locking eyes with me for longer than was comfortable.

I sighed, not wanting to hide what I was thinking. "We just need to find Chelsea."

Ames scowled and waved me off.

"Our plan will not wait to find her. We don't have that window, I'm afraid. You need to put that girl out of your mind. She's nothing but trouble," he said, sounding irritated at the mere suggestion of Chelsea.

As we were talking, I saw out of the corner of my eye someone else coming through the gate. It was a Suit, with Delphine walking close behind. She smiled when she saw us, and she walked over quickly, appearing utterly relieved to be back. I couldn't help but give her a hug—I was thrilled to see her. Like we'd said all along, we were going to do this together. We'd take Gareth and everyone in Praeclarus down once and for all.

"Are you alright?" Ames asked, looking at her, worried. Everyone hated that Delphine had been chosen by Gareth to be his lover. I didn't know if he did it to prove he could—to impress Praeclarus or what—but it was disgusting and just thinking about it made me want to kill him.

"Yeah, I'm okay," Delphine said, her green eyes cool and set with a determined stare. "Don't worry about me. I'm the last person you should be thinking about. I can take care of myself," she continued, as she pulled at her long ponytail and tapped her foot anxiously on the ground. "So, are we getting out of here or what?"

"You're one hundred percent in? Whatever happens, the die will be cast starting tonight. Are you sure you're okay with that?" Ames asked, gauging her reaction.

"Yes, of course, and now is the time to do it. Gareth doesn't suspect anything. He's completely in the dark," she said, glancing over her shoulder to make sure no one else was listening.

"How do you know that?" Ames asked, leaning in closer to her.

"Well, because I have him wrapped around my finger," Delphine said, wagging her pinky. "And I can get him to talk if I want to."

She smiled at me and I was impressed with her ease in the face of such bizarre circumstances. She always seemed unflappable, like she could handle even the most terrible things.

She was a natural athlete too—she was quicker and smarter at learning the drills than anyone else. Even when she seemed upset, she was able to shake it off quicker and easier than the rest of us.

I wondered where this well of strength and poise came from. *What was her upbringing like? How did she become the person she is today? And why the hell was she put on the Ship Out boat in the first place?* She had never shared what she had done that was so bad that her parents wanted her gone for months at a time.

Whenever I'd ask her about it, she just glossed

over her home life. She had asshole parents, just like the rest of us. She did drugs and drank too much and screwed around, just like the rest of us. She once hated her life back home, just like the rest of us.

But despite everything that she said to come across like an average girl, it felt like she was different than us. She was funnier, smarter, stronger, and the most confident. She didn't take any bullshit and everyone around her liked her. She was a cheerleader without trying. I knew I'd need her help to rally the troops when the fighting began.

And she was really pretty, in an unusual way. Delphine was odd, with a small pointed face and wild red hair and freckles, and eyes that always hinted that she was up to no good. Despite how outgoing she was, I couldn't quite understand the power she had over me.

I liked Delphine and sometimes found myself wondering what it would be like to kiss her—and then I'd push that thought out of my head and think about Chelsea. For some reason, I felt loyal to Chelsea, despite everything that had happened.

I had convinced myself that Chelsea was a product of her upbringing, but was inherently good. Her endangering herself to jump down to the Coliseum floor and publicly betray her dad made me even more certain that she was on our side now.

"So, is this going down tonight or what?" Delphine asked, looking at Ames with an accusing stare and breaking my train of thought.

Ames didn't tell us exactly when it would happen—when Elise or he would come to get me—but I was ready.

I thought about what I'd say to my dad and my mom when I'd finally get to talk to them. I hated admitting fault in anything, but now I was filled with guilt for the years of giving my parents a hard time and lying to them outright. I did a lot of bad things without any guilt whatsoever—stealing money from my dad's safe to buy drugs, and not just for me, but for all my friends. Yet I still felt angry that my parents put me in the Ship Out program.

I'd spent nights in my bed awake, trying to erase that anger. There was no room for it right now. I vowed I'd make it all right when I had a chance. None of us were perfect, but I was finally ready to admit my part in everything I'd done to my parents these past two years.

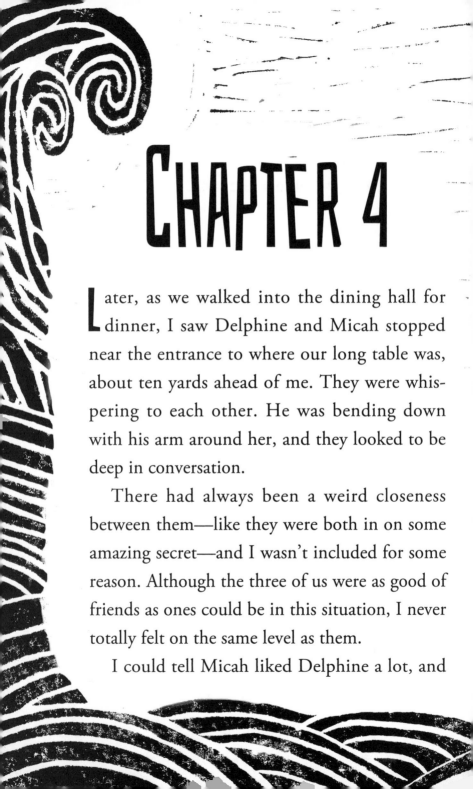

CHAPTER 4

Later, as we walked into the dining hall for dinner, I saw Delphine and Micah stopped near the entrance to where our long table was, about ten yards ahead of me. They were whispering to each other. He was bending down with his arm around her, and they looked to be deep in conversation.

There had always been a weird closeness between them—like they were both in on some amazing secret—and I wasn't included for some reason. Although the three of us were as good of friends as ones could be in this situation, I never totally felt on the same level as them.

I could tell Micah liked Delphine a lot, and

wondered if they were together and were keeping it from me. I'm not sure why they'd do that, aside from worrying I'd be jealous. But I liked Chelsea—they both knew it—and despite Delphine flirting with me just because she could, I never tried to make a move on her or anything.

I stood back and watched them for a moment before approaching. I was pretty certain Delphine was filling Micah in on what was going to go down. But, for some reason, he looked grimmer than I'd ever seen him, and Delphine leaned in and put her head against his chest. It was just a momentary gesture—a second really—I'm sure no one else saw except me.

I felt awkward approaching after catching them in that moment, so I stepped forward and cleared my throat. Micah looked embarrassed when he saw me, like I'd found them doing something far worse.

"Hey—are you guys talking about what I think you're talking about?" I asked, quiet enough to be

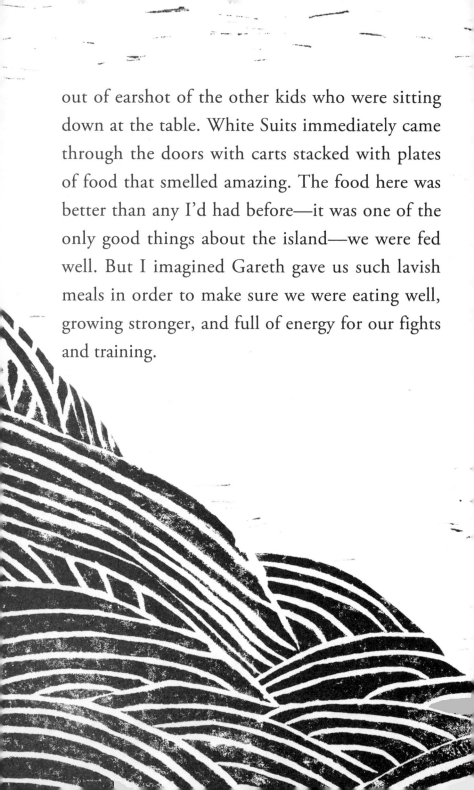

out of earshot of the other kids who were sitting down at the table. White Suits immediately came through the doors with carts stacked with plates of food that smelled amazing. The food here was better than any I'd had before—it was one of the only good things about the island—we were fed well. But I imagined Gareth gave us such lavish meals in order to make sure we were eating well, growing stronger, and full of energy for our fights and training.

CHAPTER 5

Ames made eye contact with me from across the room, and instead of ordering us to sit down and eat, which was typical, he let us linger for a moment. No one else seemed to care as they stuffed food in their mouths. The room filled with the clinking of glasses and silverware and post-training chatter.

"So—it's really starting, isn't it?" Micah asked, looking doubtful. I understood why he didn't trust that it was actually real. Ames and Elise had tried to start a revolt and failed. "How do you know this is going to work?"

"I don't," I said, shrugging and shifting my

weight nervously. For all I knew, we could be walking into some massive trap.

"It'll work, don't worry," Delphine responded, dismissing any concerns with a small wave of her hand and glaring at Micah.

"You're right," I said, trying to push away my nervousness. "I just need to talk to my dad. He'll know what to do. I'll tell him that I'm still alive and that Gareth is still alive—that alone might give him a heart attack. And then I'll let him know that a bunch of us are trapped here, that we're being killed off, and that we need his help."

"But how will he find us?" Micah asked.

"I have no idea. I don't know where we are. But he has people who can help with that. I know he'll find a way. It's our only hope. We just have to wait for Ames tonight or Elise—"

As I said it, I saw them exchange a quick, worried glance.

"What?" I asked, wondering what that was about.

"Oh. It's nothing, Reed. Don't worry about it," Delphine said, brushing me off.

"No, I saw that look you guys just gave each other, like something is wrong. What's going on?" I demanded.

"Elise is just a little batty, that's all. I hope we can trust her," Delphine said.

"Ames believes in her," I said. I had faith in Ames, so I knew we could rely on Elise too. And besides, what choice did we have? Even if Elise appeared to be a little unstable, they were a package deal and our link to help us reach the outside world.

"Now's not the time to question—"

"Okay guys!" Ames bellowed from across the room. "Let's sit and eat," he said, pointing to the empty seats and full plates at the end of the table. I bet he thought we seemed suspicious, standing there talking to each other and not eating. I looked at the six White Suits positioned around the room, each with a club in hand, and I wondered which ones were on our side, if any. Maybe they were all secretly watching us, straining to hear what we were talking about. I don't think Ames would've rushed us to sit down if he trusted that all of them were on our side. Who knew who was trying to eavesdrop?

Delphine sighed loudly and dramatically, like she was more annoyed than she actually was, and all the kids spread out at the tables laughed a bit, and then went back to eating their food.

We dug into our plates of steak, mashed potatoes, and French bread, and I reached out my fork to tap it against Micah's and Delphine's plates, getting their attention.

"You guys are going to have to rally everyone else to support us, okay?" I said under my breath, gesturing with my fork at all the other kids sitting down the table, eating cherry pie and ice cream. "They all hate me now—"

"Oh, don't worry," Delphine responded quietly, and I scanned the table to see who might be pausing to try to listen in, but no one seemed to be paying attention. "Why would they *not* support the revolt?"

"I don't know . . . fear? Or maybe Gareth will make promises to them to turn them against us," I shrugged. I knew Gareth would say anything to manipulate people to support his cause, even if they were lies.

After we sat there quietly for a moment, Ames yelled to everyone in the room, "Okay, it's time for us to head back to our rooms for bed. You all ready?"

"But we haven't had our pie!" Delphine complained, looking down the table at everyone else, whose plates were empty except for some crumbs. We had been too busy talking to eat dessert.

"You snooze you lose, my friend. We have to go," he said, nodding toward the hallway.

Delphine groaned, but we all got up and walked out the door into the long hallway that led to our barracks. Three of the Suits marched in front of our group and three walked behind us. Ames took up the rear, as he always did, ensuring that no one stepped out of line. He had to act this way in front of everyone, but I knew he wanted out of here as badly as any of us.

CHAPTER 6

In one of our private conversations, Ames had told me about his family at home. It had been years since he'd seen his wife and young boy. I wondered if his son even remembered him at all, and how they'd feel to be reunited. Maybe his wife was remarried, and maybe his kid wouldn't accept him. I thought about his son being angry for reasons he didn't even understand, just like how I was with my dad. I felt bad for Ames—he was desperate to leave, but who knew what state his family would be in when he got back.

And if Gareth lived through this, I imagined we'd all have to go into hiding. If I got out of here alive, my parents would have only one dead son instead of two, but their life as they knew it would end. They'd be at the top of Gareth's and the Praeclarus members' hit list until we successfully exposed them all.

That thought made me uneasy. Maybe it was better for the revolt to happen when Praeclarus members were on the island, after all. What if we killed them all?

But I knew that fifty world leaders couldn't just go missing without raising even bigger questions. I reminded myself that's why we had to do it now. Step one—get off the Island. Step two—expose all the Praeclarus members.

But why would anyone believe us?

All of these questions made me nervous. Getting off the island would just be the first step in a long process to real freedom, if that was even possible.

We entered the living quarters. With its stark walls and bars, it always felt cold, and a chill came over me. Before the Suits directed us to each of our cells, I glanced at Micah and Delphine one last time. Micah tilted his head in a nod and Delphine winked at me, each showing their vote of confidence for what I needed to do.

I could be caught tonight, even before reaching the security area. I was certain if that happened, Gareth would take me out to the Coliseum tomorrow and execute me there, in front of everyone, putting a stop to the revolt plans once and for all. Tonight was my night.

Because the Suits were still stationed in the center of the living quarters, I changed into the boxer shorts and white t-shirt I wore to bed. After they left, I'd change back into my normal clothes, ready to be outside in the middle of the night.

I lay in bed and the Suits finally turned off the lights. The other kids yelled at each other, joking around. It was not unusual that they weren't including me—ever since I killed Odin, they all but ignored me except when they needed something, like for me to pass the salt at the dinner table. Otherwise, outside of the training area, I might as well have been invisible.

Delphine and Micah were noticeably quiet tonight, which *was* unusual. I guessed they were willing everyone to just shut up already and go to sleep, just like me.

I was thinking that Ames was keeping tabs on our activity, waiting for everyone to crash so he could come retrieve me. We all slept deeply here— once you passed out, you were knocked out all night, exhausted from a day of training in the hot sun for hours on end.

I tossed and turned in my bed, utterly wide-awake and anxious. The other kids' dumb conversations became fewer and fewer, and everyone started to quiet, and I soon heard snoring coming from all around me. A few people were still whispering to each other through their cell bars, and just a tiny bit of moonlight shone through the windows up high on the walls.

I stared at the bars of my cell and the entrance

just beyond it and waited. Finally, it seemed like there was no movement in the space at all and snores and heavy breathing filled the black space. I was certain I was the only one still awake, aside from maybe Delphine and Micah, who were likely just as anxious as I was.

I sat up in my bed and perched on the edge, knowing Ames would be coming any minute. We didn't have a lot of time. We had to act while most Suits were surely asleep and there were only a few patrolling the grounds.

I assumed the security cameras would be shut off when he'd enter so there would be no record of my leaving or returning, and no record of us slipping through the hallways and to the security bank. We'd have to rush to make the call—and for me to tell my dad as much as I could—before anyone was alerted that something was amiss.

I knew not everyone on the security team was on our side, and that some suspected others of being disloyal to Gareth.

As I waited, it felt like forever and I wished I had a watch or clock to check the time. I stood up and began to pace the cell anxiously. Where was he? Or where was Elise?

I noticed that the sliver of moonlight was shifting, ever so slowly, across the wall. I guessed that it was the middle of the night, and I was exhausted, but wired and feeling desperate. Why weren't they coming for me?

I laid down finally, so tired, and I honestly felt like crying as the light changed from darkness to deep blue to muddy brown to gray, and everyone started to stir around me.

I looked over and saw Micah and Delphine, each in their cells a few enclosures away from me. They stared at me wide-eyed and serious—they knew I hadn't left. I could tell.

But what had happened?

CHAPTER 7

Everyone around me was getting dressed, accustomed to the daily routine. I put on a fresh pair of shorts and a tank top, and then sat at the edge of my bed, jittery from a night without sleep, and filled with anxiety.

I worried about Ames and why he hadn't shown up. And I hadn't seen Elise since the night in the medical quarters when we talked about the plan. It seemed very strange that she hadn't tried to communicate with me at all.

I couldn't talk to Delphine and Micah about it yet. I was anxious to get to a place where we could discuss, even just momentarily, to figure out what to do next. Ames and Elise were the only two staffers that I was certain were on our side. And they were the only two with the means to let me out of my cell in the middle of the night. I didn't have anyone else to trust if they'd been found out.

Unlike a normal morning, the Suits came in alone, without Ames. He usually was with them when they escorted us to the dining hall before training began. I was too scared to ask them about him because I didn't want to rouse any extra suspicions in case something had gone sideways overnight and Ames was in trouble.

Delphine piped up suddenly. "Hey . . . where's Ames?" she called out to the Suit who was standing closest to her cell. He was one of the stern ones that never made eye contact with any of us, or engaged in any form of conversation.

He shrugged in a noncommittal sort of way and didn't look in Delphine's direction. "Time for breakfast, let's go," he said, and the other Suits opened our cell doors and we all streamed out and followed them down the hallway to the dining room. The whole time, I scanned any open doors and side hallways, trying to get a glimpse of any sign of Ames or Elise—or any clue that something had gone amiss.

Everything looked normal. When I tried to get closer to Delphine and Micah, who were walking ahead of me, Delphine glanced back and a Suit quickly moved between us, blocking us from each other. I glared up at the dude, confused, but he refused to look down at me or let me step in front of him, each time blocking my body as I tried to get around him.

I sighed loudly, annoyed, but knew there was no use making a big deal of it, as it would only draw more attention to something being fishy.

In the dining hall, everyone shuffled into their normal seats and I sat across from Delphine and Micah, who both stared at me with worried grimaces, concerned. The Suit who brought our food trays over proceeded to stand just behind us as we ate.

I tried to shovel down the eggs and bacon but my stomach was in knots. I looked around the room every couple of minutes, searching for Ames or Elise.

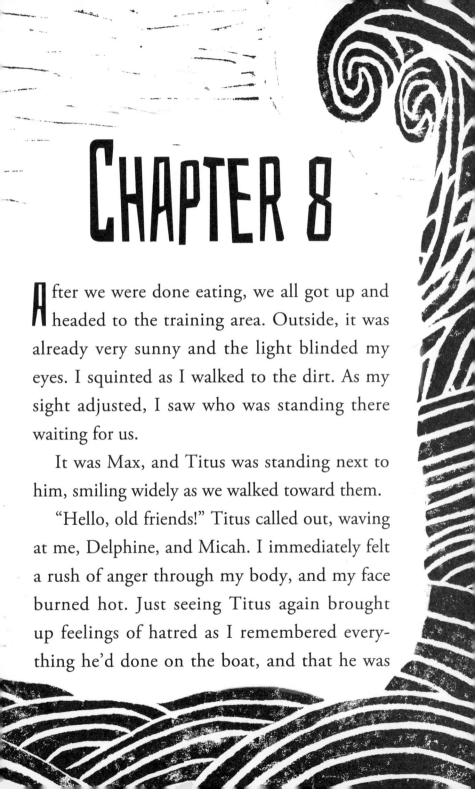

CHAPTER 8

After we were done eating, we all got up and headed to the training area. Outside, it was already very sunny and the light blinded my eyes. I squinted as I walked to the dirt. As my sight adjusted, I saw who was standing there waiting for us.

It was Max, and Titus was standing next to him, smiling widely as we walked toward them.

"Hello, old friends!" Titus called out, waving at me, Delphine, and Micah. I immediately felt a rush of anger through my body, and my face burned hot. Just seeing Titus again brought up feelings of hatred as I remembered every-thing he'd done on the boat, and that he was the one who brought me here to the island in the first place. That urge to kill suddenly rose up and I wondered what I'd do if I was ever alone with him.

"What are you doing here?" Delphine asked, sounding annoyed.

"Just taking over for a little bit," he said, with his arms crossed and with a smug look thanks to his gigantic, white smile that I'd grown to hate.

"Taking over?" Micah asked.

"Yes, from Ames for a little bit."

My heart dropped and I tried not to panic. *What was happening?*

I couldn't help myself.

"Where's Ames?" I asked.

"He had a little accident last night," Max said. "He drank a little too much—stress relief, I think—and whoops, he fell down the stairs leading to his flat."

"It was ugly," Titus interrupted. "So, here I am, filling in to take care of you rug rats while he recovers."

I was sure it was a lie, of course, but what was I supposed to say or do? I was just hoping that Ames was still alive. Had we been found out? And if so, who discovered us? And what would Ames's punishment be? I felt desperate and uncertain of what I could possibly do now.

Titus looked pleased at this turn of events. It was as if his one life mission was to make me miserable, and now that he was in charge of our training he would be able to fulfil that goal. "As you all know, Praeclarus members will be coming back soon and training can't stop just because Ames is injured, now can it?" he asked.

A few people around me grumbled, including Delphine and Micah, but I was silent. I was fuming—we were so close! I wasn't going to let this stop me. I'd just need to figure out how to escape and get to the security bank on my own.

We went through training and the rage I felt inside kept on building with each minute that passed. I wrestled this kid named Junior, who was huge and usually a good opponent, but I was furious and instead of just pinning him down, I started punching him. I hit him in the face as hard as I could, repeatedly. He squinted up at me, confused, as he tried to shield his face with his hands.

"What are you doing, dude?" he yelled out in his thick accent.

Titus and Max were at once behind me, pulling me off of him. They tossed me aside and I fell to the ground with a hard, painful thump, my knees scraping against the dirt.

"Take it easy!" Delphine came over and looked down at me, annoyed. "You gotta control yourself, Reed," she said, as she bent down to help lift me up. "Don't worry. We'll figure this out together," she whispered in my ear, and I wished I could be anywhere else. I bit my lip and stood up, wiping the dirt off my shirt and glaring at Titus and Max.

"I'm cool. Sorry man," I said to Junior. "I'm not sure what came over me."

"It's okay. It's okay . . . " he said, wiping the

blood dripping from his nose with the back of his hand. "This place gets the best of us all."

I could see the rest of the kids standing back, watching me and scowling.

"Yeah," I said, trying to shake it off. I needed to keep my cool. Delphine was right.

I walked over to get a sip of water at the fountain and looked back. Delphine came trotting over, and I was surprised that Titus didn't stop her from running over to talk to me, like the Suits had done this morning.

"Are you okay?" she asked, and reached over and wiped some dirt off my face with a delicate brush of her fingers. I felt a jolt of electricity go through me, and I could tell I was starting to turn red.

She smiled at me, like she felt my embarrassment immediately.

"Aww, Reed, I thought your heart was with Chelsea?" she teased me, and I knew it was silly.

Why the hell was I feeling anything toward any girls at all?

"You have to keep your head in the game, Reed," she continued, gripping my shoulder with her little hand. "This is not the time to get soft. You have a plan, don't you?" she looked at me expectantly, and it almost felt like she was taunting me.

"Yes, I do. It's all good," I said.

"Yes, that's true. Good things come to those who have faith that it will all work out," she said.

"Are you sure about that?" I asked, feeling doubtful. The sun was burning my neck, and I really just wanted to go lie down in a cool place and go to sleep. My body was out of whack from staying up all night.

"No, but it sure sounded good, right?" she joked in her sarcastic way. She slapped me on the butt hard before turning and jogging back to where everyone else was sitting, holding their arms over their foreheads to try to shade their faces from the blinding rays of the sun.

I'd do anything—anything—to be back home right at that instant. To be in my bedroom, on my red flannel sheets, staring up at the ceiling with nothing to do. Or to be at wrestling practice, the monotony of practice with no dire consequences to face. And I would've done anything to see my mom again—to sit with her at our kitchen counter while she made an espresso and I ate cereal and we talked about the dumb stuff that used to preoccupy my life. Or to see my dad again, and to try to get to know him, and to ask him to get to know me. It had been a long time since we'd been honest with each other, since we'd had a real talk, or thrown a ball together, or sat and chatted about the newspaper or about sports. I realized that that was both of our faults, and I was ready to take responsibility for my part of it.

I thought about all my friends and what they must be doing right at that very moment. I tried to guess what time it was in Portland right now, but had no idea. Were they all sleeping in their beds? Were they at parties? *They must all think I'm dead now*, I realized. I wondered if they'd had a funeral for me, and what people said about me. I'd been such a shithead to so many of them. What could they possibly say about me that I'd actually want to hear, or believe was the truth?

I walked back to the group, trying not to look too glum, feeling everyone staring at me.

"You ready to continue, Reed?" Titus asked, and I knew there wasn't a choice. If I resisted, I'd probably be thrown into solitary confinement and then I really couldn't do anything at that point.

"Yes," I said. "What's next?"

Titus's face twisted up into a smile. "Good boy. I'd knew you'd come around."

We went through more exercises and Micah insisted he be matched up against me. Titus shrugged, agreeing. Micah was probably doing this to protect me from acting like an asshole or idiot to anyone else. We grappled against each other and my heart wasn't in it, but I pretended anyway, not wanting to draw more attention to myself.

He pinned me down easily. "Man, you're making this too easy for me. This is valuable time to get stronger, remember?" he asked, and I nodded, wiping sweat from my forehead with the corner of my shirt.

At the end of the day, we retreated to our cells and I wondered where Ames and Elise were being held and if I'd ever see them again.

Even though I was uneasy, I changed and lay down in my bed and fell asleep, dead tired. I hadn't slept at all the night before and I couldn't help it. My eyes were heavy and I ignored the yelling of everyone around me—the annoying nightly cat calls and teasing—and passed out, just wanting to forget where I was for a few hours and hope that when I woke up, Ames would be back and we'd have a plan for what to do.

In the middle of the night, when all else was silent and everyone was still, I felt something poke me. I rolled over, confused, forgetting where I was momentarily. I pushed the thing away and grunted, and something poked me in my side again, this time much harder.

I turned over in bed and opened my eyes. It was nearly pitch black but as my sight adjusted, I recognized Chelsea standing on the other side of the bars.

I couldn't see her that well, but she put her finger up to her lips to make sure I was being quiet. I didn't dare make a sound.

CHAPTER 9

Chelsea went over to my cell door and very, very slowly put in the code, turned the handle, and pulled the door open enough for me to slide through. She didn't say anything, but grabbed me and tugged me out the door. A Suit was standing there, but he didn't make eye contact with me or acknowledge us at all. Chelsea led me away, and I wondered where she was taking me.

We went down the hallway that led to the outdoors and it was very hard to see. The few lights along the outdoor corridor were dim and I didn't see anyone else around.

She led me further from the doorway to a

dark patch between two of the lights, and I could barely make out the shape of her in the inky night.

She reached over and pulled me into a hug. It was a firm, long grasp and she didn't move at all, like she was clinging to me for dear life. I heard her breathing heavily and I felt her tremble. I wrapped my arms around her tightly and we stood like that for what felt like several minutes, when it was likely just seconds. If we were anywhere else it would feel romantic, but in that moment I was confused as to what was happening.

"What's going on? Where have you been?"

"I've been in solitary confinement in a cell carved into the mountainside, away from absolutely everyone. I knew my dad would put me there once I was led away."

"What do you mean? Where'd he take you?" I asked.

"Very few people know about that cell. It's tucked away. My dad knew some people would help me escape if they found me."

"Really? Who?"

"We have people on our side, Reed. We just need to get to them."

"I know. We were about to reach out to my dad, but Ames disappeared."

"I know all about that, and about Elise," she said, and although I couldn't see her, I could hear her voice quiver like she was about to start crying.

"What about Elise?"

"Oh. I can't believe you don't know. I thought you would've heard already."

"Heard what?"

"She was killed, Reed," she said.

I pulled away from our embrace. "What? What do you mean? I just saw her a few days ago." I was totally confused.

"Gareth killed her. After all this time, he'd finally had enough. That's all I know for sure," she said.

"Wait . . . how do you know that?" I asked, not understanding. "You've been locked away."

"Jacob told me. And they got to Ames too," she said urgently, and I heard her sniffling. I squinted to try to see her in the darkness.

"Who's Jacob? And what do you mean they got to Ames?"

"Ames is alive, but they stopped him from reaching you. Who knows what Gareth will do to him in the long run. Anyway, I have to get back. But when Jacob comes for you, you have to trust him."

"What? I don't understand? Who is he?"

"He's the head of security—the one you were supposed to see. But we can't talk more about it now. The most important thing you should know now is to trust Jacob. We have to return before anyone on Gareth's team realizes we are missing. I had a short window, and I must go now—"

"To where?"

"To my jail cell, Reed," she said plainly.

"But why don't you just hide out somewhere

else? Don't you know this island backward and forward?" I asked.

"Yes, but if I went missing, Gareth would hunt for me until he found me, and he knows this island better than even I do. I could only hide for so long."

"You won't have to hide long. We're going to revolt soon," I said.

"I know. That's why I need to bide my time. Then, when the right moment comes, Jacob and you will help me get out, and I'll leave this place with you," she said.

She grabbed my hand and drew me under the light momentarily. She looked so pretty, with her dark hair falling into her face. I leaned in to kiss her, but she pulled away and turned to start walking away.

"It's time for us to get back. We can't be gone too long."

"Wait . . . " I tried to say, but she shushed me as we headed toward my living quarters. The same

Suit was standing there and he nodded at Chelsea. It was obvious to me now that he was on our side and that he was helping her out, standing guard for us.

She didn't say another word as she led me to my cell and closed the door quietly behind me. And just like that, she was gone again.

CHAPTER 10

I listened to try to detect if anyone was stirring, paranoid that someone heard us depart or come back in. But it was completely silent except for the rhythmic sounds of everyone breathing.

If it was true that Elise had been killed, that meant that Gareth definitely knew about our plan. Why else had he kept her alive for so many years—when she'd gone against his will and not supported him and his endeavors—to just kill her now? I had a bad feeling that we had been found out and that was also why Ames was taken away from us.

But I had a glimmer of hope now. Just a tiny

bit. Chelsea was alive and okay, relatively speaking, and I had a name of someone else that could help us—Jacob—the person I needed to see, in fact. The one who would connect me to my dad.

I would have to wait for him to find me, and I had no idea when or how he'd reach me. Despite all of our history, I trusted Chelsea. She truly acted like she wanted out of here as much as any of us.

I wondered where she'd go if she got off the island. This was the only place she'd ever known. I thought about asking her if she'd want to come to Oregon, and wondered if it was silly for me to even think that. My parents would help her—I knew they would—even if she was Gareth's daughter. I was excited to talk to her about the possibility the next time I got to see her.

I fell asleep, knowing Jacob would likely not come that night and that I'd have to be patient.

The next morning at breakfast, I felt lighter on my feet and I was eager to talk to Delphine and Micah about this development, but the Suits stood guard next to us again. There was no way I could speak freely.

"You're in a good mood," Delphine said as she ate her oatmeal. She raised her eyebrows. "What's going on?"

I nodded toward the Suits and shook my head. "Not much. Another day in paradise, that's all." I smiled up at a Suit who was staring at me.

"Hmm . . . " Delphine said skeptically, and gave Micah a look. He just rolled his eyes at her and then grinned.

"What day of the week is it?" I asked, glancing at the Suit again.

He glared at me but didn't say anything. They were expected to speak to us as little as possible. Suits weren't allowed to make connections with us. They were here as muscle and that's it—not sounding boards, not buddies, not anything but nameless bodies to keep us in line.

"I think it's a Monday?" Delphine guessed, shrugging her shoulders.

"Yeah, I have no idea, man," Micah said.

"That sounds right," I said, thinking about the week ahead.

I couldn't share more. If that was true, the Praeclarus people would be arriving in five days. They always arrived on Saturdays and Sundays, like clockwork. New shipments of food and sundries came in a few days before, staff prepped everything before the weekend, and then visitors started arriving on Saturday mornings. Although I couldn't keep track of how many days had passed since our arrival, I knew that that one rule always held true.

If we were going to try to enact the plan before Praeclarus started showing up, Jacob would likely come find me soon. I just needed to stay out of trouble and alive until then.

I could tell Delphine wanted to say more to me but we couldn't speak freely at the moment. I was excited to share with her the development about Jacob.

Just like she had told me, all hope was not lost. She was always right, I realized. She stared at me as if she was reading my mind and smirked.

"Let's go to practice now," she said. She stood up, stretched her arms above the group, and started to lead everyone outdoors, with Titus and Max alongside.

Titus put his arm around Delphine and she tried to pull away, glaring at him.

"So—I hear you're Gareth's special friend, aren't you?" he asked.

"None of your business," she spat back at him, trying to push him off of her, which made him laugh.

"I've always liked you, Delphine," he said. "From the very beginning. I could tell you have a certain spunk—and that you're not like anyone else," he continued. "Isn't that right, Delphine?"

"Whatever you say, Titus," she said, brushing him off.

"You're something else. No wonder Gareth likes

you so much. I hear you get extra-special treatment from him, don't you?" he persisted, grabbing her even tighter as we walked along the corridor to the training area.

"Back off," I muttered behind them, and Titus eyed me, annoyed.

"Oh, stop. Delphine and I are just having a little fun. She can take it, right, Delphine?"

"Oh yeah, don't worry about me, Reed," she said. "Titus just likes to give me a hard time. I think he may be jealous of Gareth's affection," she teased.

Micah snickered and Titus was quiet before finally starting to laugh too. I was confused. They seemed to be ribbing each other good-naturedly. What was going on?

When we got to the training area, I saw that Gareth was already there, sitting in the tall purple chair overlooking the proceedings. *What is he doing here?* I wondered. Whenever he was around, that meant something was up, and it was never a good sign.

"Hello, Gareth!" Titus called out as we entered. He was not surprised to see him.

"Sir!" Gareth said in return, smiling widely, his straight white teeth, tanned skin, and perfect hair making him look like an aging movie star. He exuded confidence and charm, like someone people always listened to when he spoke.

"How are my children doing?" Gareth asked, and I felt myself cringe. "Have they all been behaving? I sometimes get the feeling that a few of you are very bad, and always up to no good," he said as he looked us over. We were standing just below him now. I stared back, not wanting to give him even a hint that I might be involved in any sort of trouble at all.

"My tolerance for disobedience is getting lower and lower. In fact, I wanted to show you all something—"

He pointed to the large screen at the end of the

training area. It hadn't been used since we arrived and I had wondered what it was for.

He aimed his wristlet at it and it lit up. The screen went from black to blue and suddenly a grotesque image of a dead woman splayed out in an open grave was on the screen.

The woman's arms and legs were twisted unnaturally and her hair was spread across her face. But the shot zoomed in and I could see clearly through the tangled mess that it was Elise. She gazed up at the camera with a blank, glassy stare.

I had seen so many dead bodies, but that image shocked me and made me feel sick.

We were all silent, and I was unable to look away.

"Poor Elise. I was patient with her for so long. For years I tried to look the other way when she repeatedly betrayed me. I loved her. I really did, her being the mother of my dear daughter, after all—"

Wait. What? I couldn't believe what he was

telling us—Elise was Chelsea's mom? Did she know that? I didn't think so and I felt devastated for her.

"You see—this is what happens to the mother of my only child when she betrays me one too many times. And I feel much, much less for each of you," he continued, still smiling, but looking a little sad. "I've invested a lot in all of you—invaluable training time, money spent to feed and house you. I've rescued many of you from lives on the streets or from lives as drug addicts. And now, look. You're at your physical peak and more powerful than you'd ever be without me. Death is inevitable for all of us, but I've given you the gift of strength, power, and skill—something none of you had before—"

What a load of garbage, I thought.

"Well, except you, Delphine, my love. You are extraordinary through and through, and I suspect that's the way you've always been," he said, sounding all of a sudden like a love-struck teenager.

I saw Micah smirk out of the corner of my eye, and was surprised Gareth's words didn't cause him to lunge forward and try to strangle Gareth right then and there.

"And, well, let me show you someone else who got a little too wound up, and on my dime, too—someone who had been pretty loyal to a point, which makes his latest transgressions come as a bit of a shock to me. Ames, come out," Gareth commanded, and I looked to the training entrance. Two Suits were walking in, flanking Ames.

I almost didn't recognize him—the man who was being dragged in was completely black and blue, his eyes swollen nearly shut, and his arms hanging limply at his sides.

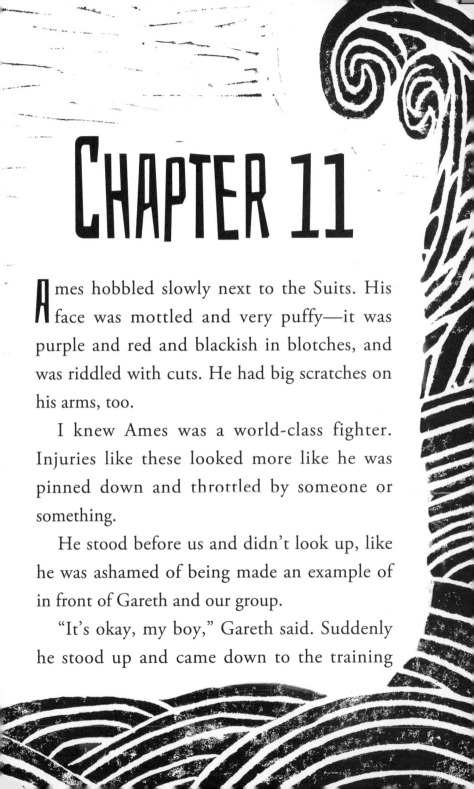

CHAPTER 11

Ames hobbled slowly next to the Suits. His face was mottled and very puffy—it was purple and red and blackish in blotches, and was riddled with cuts. He had big scratches on his arms, too.

I knew Ames was a world-class fighter. Injuries like these looked more like he was pinned down and throttled by someone or something.

He stood before us and didn't look up, like he was ashamed of being made an example of in front of Gareth and our group.

"It's okay, my boy," Gareth said. Suddenly he stood up and came down to the training floor—something he'd never done before. I could reach out and kill him—snap his neck in an instant, I realized. I thought about it, but saw the Suits standing next to Ames had their left hands resting on guns in their holsters, and thought better of it.

What was Gareth doing, coming down here?

He walked over to Ames and pulled him in for a hug, putting his arms around him and squeezing him tight. He rested his chin on Ames's shoulder and pressed his nose practically against Ames's ear. I could see Ames wince, but he didn't dare shift— like he feared a sudden movement would change the dynamic completely.

Gareth whispered something in Ames's ear, who nodded slowly and said "Okay," before Gareth pulled away.

When he separated from Ames and turned to face us, I saw splotches of Ames's blood had stained Gareth's shirt and pants. He glanced down at it and looked disgusted.

"Titus, you're relieved of your duties here. Go back to your other post, please. You've been missed over there," Gareth said. And then, without any more speeches, he turned to leave, with the Suits trailing him. *Where was Titus posted?*

Titus looked annoyed, and Delphine couldn't help herself. "See ya, Titus! You're not wanted here!"

He glared at her, snapped his sunglasses off of his face, and walked through the doors leading to the corridor away from the training area.

We were left standing there just with Ames, Max, and the rest of the kids, and all were quiet for a moment. I could sense that Ames needed to collect himself for a second.

"Are you okay?" I finally asked, breaking the silence.

"I'll be alright. Just another beautiful day," he said, waving dismissively at his surroundings. He looked broken, like he had been put through a special kind of hell. This was a former special operations fighter. He had described his training to me before, and I knew he was accustomed to being pushed past the level of physical discomfort, and that he had endured pain on a regular basis as part of his training.

But he now stood before us, utterly defeated and spooked, like he had seen a ghost. I wondered why Gareth hadn't killed him outright like he had done to Elise, and I couldn't help but speak up.

"Why are you even still alive?" I asked.

"That's a story for another time—especially when it's time to get started, isn't it?" Ames asked, and he barely looked at us. "Let's begin with laps. You know the drill." He spoke each word slowly, as if speaking hurt, and he waved us off before hobbling over to the wall and leaning against it, exhausted.

We skipped sideways, scissoring our legs to the front and to the back, and Delphine jogged up next to me. "What do you think happened?"

"I think they found out we're trying to escape and they beat the shit out of him," I said.

"Yeah, that sounds about right. What a bummer," she responded, like it was no big deal, and then ran ahead of me, taking the lead. I didn't know if she was unfazed or just didn't want to show any weakness in front of everyone.

CHAPTER 12

Later in the day's training, right before lunch, I stepped aside to stretch and I asked Ames to come talk to me. I stood in the corner and I saw Delphine and Micah watching us.

I waved them off when they started to approach to join the conversation. Ames seemed off and I didn't want to overwhelm him—I needed to find out what happened and what the next steps were, now that the timing of our plan was completely out of whack.

He limped over and before I had a chance to say anything, he hissed at me.

"The plan is off, we have to call off the dogs—"

"What?"

"We have to lay low. Gareth's on to us and I need to rethink everything."

"What do you mean?"

"He tried to get me to tell him who on his security team was working against him, but I refused to share anything, which is why I look like I do—"

"So, did he know that the revolt was imminent?"

"No, I don't think so. But he knows that people have been messing with his security system, and he doesn't trust anyone anymore."

"Good."

"Not good. It's making him extra paranoid. And he's going to do what he needs to do to protect himself and the Island, so we need to hold off—"

"No, we can't! I'll be dead if I have to go back into the Coliseum. You know that. I can't face one of the Creatures again."

"You'll be dead if we try to do this without

having a new plan in place. The only reason I'm still alive is because Gareth thinks I have an 'in' with the security team and is threatening my life so I can get to the bottom of it. Now's not the time—I need to come up with a different plan."

"Please, Ames!" I couldn't help but plead and I glanced over and saw people looking over at us, including Delphine and Micah.

"Besides, I need to discuss everything with Elise," Ames said. "I can't do anything until I talk to her about this."

He didn't know yet. *Crap.*

"Ames. You're going to need to be quiet, but I'm about to tell you something horrible. It's awful . . . Elise is dead."

He gazed down at me, his face bloated and discolored, and his mouth hung open.

"No. That can't be. What are you talking about?" he asked quietly, taking my cue not to make a scene.

"Before you came into the training area, Gareth showed us a video—of Elise in a grave."

"That can't be right. Gareth loves Elise. He always has . . . " His words trailed off, as if the news was just truly hitting him.

"I promise you. We saw it with our own eyes in a video. It wasn't a lie. Gareth told us that she betrayed him one too many times."

"I don't understand—" Ames said, and held onto my shoulder tightly, as if he was trying not to collapse to the ground.

"Keep it together, Ames—they're all watching," I said, and continued to stretch.

"I don't believe that he'd kill her, but not me. It doesn't make sense." He ran a swollen hand through his hair and sighed. "I'm definitely next if I can't give him the info he's looking for." I knew this was probably true. "That's why we have to come up with a new plan right away. I'm afraid Gareth's paranoia is causing him to unravel. I think he'll do whatever it takes to protect the

Island, even if it means taking everything out at once."

"I know—" he said. "Let me think about it. I need to speak to Jacob."

"Jacob! Yes! Chelsea told me about him," I could see Delphine and Micah approaching, and they wouldn't stop, even though I tried to wave them away.

"Hey. Keep this all to yourself, okay?" Ames said, "Not a word, even to them," he whispered, managing to smile as they approached.

"Yikes! You've looked better. Are you okay?" Delphine asked, and Ames managed a small laugh.

"Oh just fine. I have to get back to work. Excuse me," he said. He made eye contact with me as he walked away.

"What was that about, man?" Micah asked. "Is he feeling alright?"

I glanced up at them. "Yeah, I think so. He's just really shaken up."

"Did you guys talk about the plan? What's the update?" Delphine asked. "We can't wait . . ."

I thought about Jacob, about Elise, and about Ames asking me not to say anything, even to my only real friends here. I would tell them, just not right now. I felt like I was betraying him.

"We didn't have a chance to talk. He's pretty shaken up." I tried to sound as non-committal as possible. I felt guilty. I'd never held anything back from them before, but it felt like the right thing to do in the moment.

"Are you not telling us something, Reed?" Delphine asked.

"What? No," I said, annoyed that she was insinuating something that was indeed actually true.

"Well, I just hope he's not too shaken to make a new plan." She pulled me in for a playful hug and Micah tousled my hair.

"He's our last hope," Delphine said.

"I know. Hopefully we can talk again once he's

in his right mind," I said, trying to assure them so they'd get off my back.

"Totally. Good idea," Micah agreed. "We shouldn't push him. God knows what a horrible thing he just went through."

As we went back to the area where everyone else sat, I wondered what my fellow fighters were thinking.

When could we start to rally all the other kids against Gareth? It would be risky to do it too early, before we had a concrete way to escape. What if someone talked, or spoke too loudly about our secrets in front of the Suits, or what if fighting broke out when we had no way to leave? What would happen then?

I had memorized a list in my head of all the Praeclarus members. Just like the memories of my brother that I categorized in lists, I was memorizing who they were. I wanted to be ready to expose them to the world when the time came.

I knew Ames had to talk to Jacob right

away—things would get a lot more complicated once the Praeclarus members came. They were going to start arriving by helicopters and boats from other locations on Saturday—that would add another thirty to forty people to fight against.

That night, I waited, sure that Ames was going to do the right thing and find a way to communicate to Jacob, and that one of them would come find me.

Sure enough, I heard someone enter and got up to see who it was. It was Ames.

I glanced around. It didn't seem like anyone else was awake. Ames led me outside. The whole room was still except for us, and I was relieved that I wouldn't have to try to explain this to anyone the next morning.

Ames took me out through the dimly lit hallway and turned to look at me once we were in earshot.

"What have you told anybody about our plan?" he demanded.

"Nothing. Well, nothing new since Delphine and I talked to Elise. There is no plan, remember?"

"So, you haven't said anything about Jacob to anyone—even Delphine or Micah?"

"No," which was true, but honestly, I just hadn't had the chance to yet. "But do you know who told me about Jacob and that I should trust him? Chelsea."

"Yes, Jacob told me that Chelsea knows about him," Ames said, frowning, and like he was deep in thought. He finally continued, "No one else must know about Jacob—no one—even people you think you can trust. That is a very, very closely guarded secret. You understand?"

"Yes," I said, nodding. He was crystal clear.

"Good. Your ability to get out of here alive depends on Jacob connecting you to your dad. And if anyone knows that Jacob is the ring leader of the security breach, we're all dead."

"Okay, I understand," I said. "So, what is

happening right now? Why did you take me outside tonight? Is tonight the night?"

"Yes, you guessed it. I'm taking you to see Jacob. We're going to contact your dad tonight," he said, matter-of-factly. I was relieved.

"Why'd you change your mind?" I asked.

"I came to my senses that my time is limited here. Gareth will want to take me out when I can't give up specific secrets on the issues with security. I don't have a lot of time and will just have to try to stall him. And, if Elise and Chelsea weren't safe from Gareth's punishment, why would I be any different?" he asked.

I was thankful things were in motion. Tonight was the night to take the first real steps toward the beginning of the revolt.

CHAPTER 13

"So, are we safe tonight?" I asked, scanning for movement to make sure no one was coming.

"Yes, don't worry. For months we've been rearranging the staff assignments randomly to throw Gareth off on who might be involved in our plans. We reassign people to different posts—especially overnight—sometimes with Gareth's people and sometimes with our people—so we can strategize when to gather smaller pockets of our group to pass on messages and so forth."

"And tonight is one of those nights?" I asked. I didn't see any other Suits anywhere but I knew they were out there.

"Yes. They're stationed everywhere, but they are the guys on our side. They're watching out for us."

"But what about Gareth?" I asked, concerned that he was also out there, and could stumble upon us as we traveled to Jacob.

"Even Gareth has to sleep, right?" He chuckled. "And that's a guy who values his beauty sleep. Always has. It's amazing to me that he can sleep so soundly despite everything that he's done and the violence he witnesses every day." Ames shook his head in disbelief. "But we can't just sit here and chit chat. We have to go," he said, and he hobbled up the path that led toward the mountain.

He was still injured and he didn't walk with the same ease and confidence as before. He saw the concern in my eyes.

"Oh, don't worry about me. I'm fine," he said, as if he was reading my mind. I wondered what Gareth had done to him. If it was a regular old-fashioned beating, or if something more torturous and sinister had been involved.

As we went up the path, I searched the hills for any trail markers that might point the way to Chelsea's cell. The walkway we were on had several forks that led to other areas of the island, but Ames moved with purpose, not talking any longer. I wanted to ask questions, but knew it wasn't the time. We were on a mission with no time to discuss everything.

The overhead lights were very dim, as if someone turned them down, and it was difficult to see. Ames didn't need a flashlight, though, and walked purposefully, without hesitation.

I tried to memorize where we were going as he wound us through fork after fork toward an area of the Island I'd definitely never been to before. We were surrounded by tall, dark trees and it felt like the vegetation was closing in all around us. It was as if the trees were alive and that they were stretching out overhead to strangle all the sky's natural light. I tried not to stumble as I felt rocks and roots underfoot.

Finally, in the distance, I saw a small concrete bunker atop a hill. It was brightly lit from the inside, the only light visible from this vantage point.

I could hear Ames breathing heavily, the walk taxing him. Suddenly, a Suit popped out from the bushes. I could barely see in the darkness, but the flash of white pants and jacket were unmistakable.

"Hey! What are you doing?" Ames yelled, and I could scarcely make out the Suit lifting something above his head.

"I can't let you do this!" the man yelled. "You're going to bring down the whole Island!" he screamed, and moved toward Ames.

I saw him about to bring his arm down and I lunged forward, throwing the man to the ground. As he struggled, I punched him in the head and then the face, and then I couldn't stop myself, hitting him repeatedly. There was no way I was going to let this person stop us from getting out of here.

I felt Ames on top of me, pulling me off of him. "Don't kill him," he said sternly.

"Why not?" I asked, pausing before I pummeled him again.

"We need to know who he's working with. He used to be on our side but now he's a traitor, right, Lionel?" Ames looked down with disgust at the guy, who was now groaning in pain on the ground.

"You're the traitor!" he groaned. Even though it was dark, I could see that I'd bloodied his face and knocked out a front tooth.

"Lionel, I'm disappointed in you. I thought I knew you and I thought you knew me. You cross me and I'll fuck you," Ames said. "I'll leave you to be eaten by the Creatures when we get out of here." Ames turned to me. "C'mon, now help me get him up."

We lifted Lionel, propped his arms over our shoulders, and dragged him slowly up the hill toward the bunker. He squirmed under our grasp, but he was a Suit, not an athlete or fighter, and he didn't have the ability to fight against us.

"Who are you working with, Lionel?" Ames asked. Lionel didn't say anything. "Are you a lone wolf, or is this something more calculated?"

Lionel stayed silent.

"What are we going to do with him?" I asked.

"We'll lock him away until he talks, or if he doesn't talk, he'll just stay locked away until the revolt. And then when we leave the Island, it's every man for himself here—either imprisoned or loose with the Creatures. Lionel, I can leave that up to you—"

Lionel still didn't respond. I wondered if he was the only traitor, or if there were more. We'd have to be very careful, not knowing who was really on our side.

CHAPTER 14

We carried Lionel up to the door and it swung open. A wiry man with pale skin and an anxious demeanor greeted us.

"I've been waiting for you. What took you so long?" And then he looked at Lionel with disgust. "And what happened here?"

"Well, I think Lionel here was having second thoughts. So now we have to deal with him, too."

"Okay, well, just put him in these for the moment," the man said, pulling handcuffs from a drawer. Ames slapped them on Lionel's wrists and pushed him into the corner to sit down.

"Now be quiet. We have work to do," the man said to Lionel, who scowled up at him.

"Reed, this is Jacob. Jacob—you know Reed," Ames said.

"What do you mean?" I asked.

"Well, he doesn't know you but he's watched your every move since you arrived here," Ames said, pointing to a long wall of screens and computers that crossed the entire room—probably one hundred screens of various sizes.

The computers and monitors were showing what seemed to be every room and area on the whole Island. They were switching to different angles every couple of seconds.

"Is this live?" I asked, understanding that our every movement was being tracked. I had guessed this, but it was freaky to see it for myself.

"Right now, only some of the screens are live. Others are canned to just look like they are live—to give you guys the ability to walk around freely, and for you to get out of your cell truly

undetected," Jacob explained. He walked over to a screen toward the top right of the wall and pointed at it.

"Look at that," he instructed, and I spotted on the screen a small cell, the camera zooming in on it from above. I saw a person sleeping sprawled out in a bed, arms and legs splayed and the blanket barely covering them.

I looked closer.

"Wait—is that me?" I asked, confused.

"Ha, you're catching on," Jacob said, rolling his eyes, like I was an idiot.

"But the time stamp says right now—" I noticed, looking up at the digital clock on the wall and what was on the screen.

"Yes, that's been digitally altered, just in case."

"Just in case of what?" I asked, not understanding.

"Well, in case Gareth asks to see tapes during times I've been on duty. Then I have a record of everything looking completely normal."

"And what about him?" I asked, pointing over at another guy who was slumped over in his chair, sleeping. He was snoring very loudly.

Jacob and Ames laughed.

"That's Don. He has a bad case of narcolepsy," Jacob said, giggling.

"Or at least that's what he thinks," Ames replied.

"We slip him a little sleepy juice in his coffee sometimes and he passes out for hours," Jacob explained.

"When he wakes up, he genuinely thinks he fell asleep on the job."

"And he's too ashamed to ask for help with his embarrassing little problem. He thinks Gareth will delegate him to the life of a Suit or worse—so we keep that little secret between us," Jacob said, shaking his head like he almost felt bad for the guy.

"But why?" I asked.

"Because we don't trust Don. He has a huge mouth. And more importantly, he's loyal to

Gareth. He's on the security team, but he cannot have any access to what we are doing here. If he figured it out, Gareth would know immediately."

"Are you sure he's really knocked out?" I asked, skeptical.

"Oh, yes, we can actually move him around and when he wakes up and he has no idea what happened—it's kind of like being a blackout drunk," Jacob said.

"Which I'm sure you'll understand, isn't that right, Reed?" Ames asked, fixing me with a serious gaze. He'd originally been brought to the Island under the pretense of helping kids get clean, and I think he still felt an obligation to help guide me in some way.

"I have no idea what you mean," I joked. I looked at all the screens, scanning everything to try to get as much information as possible. "And can you see inside Gareth's room?" I asked.

"Oh, no, not there. Just outside. We can tell if anyone tries to approach that is not supposed to, so we can contact our insiders, if needed. But inside his room and his living quarters? No." Jacob said.

"I shudder to think what goes on inside of there, don't you?" Ames said.

It was true—thinking about him and Delphine and whomever else he brought to his room was horrible. It was entirely possible that he had even stranger proclivities than the ones we already knew about.

"And what about the Creatures? Can you watch them? Where are they being held?"

"They're in the hangar on the other side of the island—" Jacob said. "We have no access to video over there, so they were quite a surprise to us. I assume that's run by a whole different security detail."

"Yes, we always wondered what Gareth was doing in there, but we could never get access and Gareth would never explain," Ames said. "And now we know why, don't we?"

"But who runs that area? There have to be

people that developed the Creatures, right? And that care for them?" I asked, feeling worried there were even more people that were unaccounted for and that we'd need to fight when the time came. Plus, they had the advantage of having access to the Creatures, which they could let loose on us at will.

"Well, yes, we've identified this as a problem area—a weakness—" Jacob conceded.

"We've long suspected that there might be more barracks and people on the other side of the hangar. But we're not certain, as we've never been able to see past the hangar building itself," Ames said. "But after the Creatures were debuted, that certainly let us know that Gareth has additional people there bringing that operation to life and managing it."

"I have some ideas on how to take care of the hangar—don't worry," Jacob said, smiling. Ames nodded at him, like they shared a secret they wouldn't let me in on.

"So, how many extra people could be over there?" I asked.

"We have no idea, but I'd say a project like that isn't some small endeavor. There are likely at least twenty scientists and staff, if not more people supporting it. How Gareth's kept them hidden away all this time, I have no idea—" Ames said.

I felt anxious doing the math. There were about fifty staffers supposedly on our side—but then, Lionel had turned on us, so who knew how many were actually going to join us when fighting began. And then there were probably around one hundred other staffers on Gareth's side, and then those who likely inhabited the unknown area by the hangar, and the Creatures themselves. The odds felt stacked against us.

"So, what is the plan, exactly?" I asked, my uneasiness taking over.

"To disable all the Island's security systems at precisely the right time to let everyone out. Then, to get weapons in the right hands at the right time.

And, most importantly, to hope to hell your dad actually has the resources to find us and to bring us a boat or helicopters to get all of us out of here alive," Ames said, looking at me.

"So, are you ready to reach out to him?" Jacob asked, as his glasses slipped down the bridge of his nose.

CHAPTER 15

"Of course I'm ready. But I need you guys to promise me something first—"

Jacob glanced at Ames with an exasperated look.

"What is it, Reed?" Ames asked, irritation in his voice.

"I need you to promise that you'll take me to Chelsea after we call my dad, and that you'll help get her out when the fighting begins."

"She's Gareth's daughter. I know you both like her, but I'd be careful," Ames warned. "I don't think the apple falls too far from the tree. I've seen her do questionable things, to you included."

"I know. But I believe that she's changed and that she'll fight with us if we give her the shot," I persisted.

"I don't think that's a good idea, Reed," Ames said.

"I will only cooperate with this plan if you agree to those terms."

I felt firm about this condition. I needed to speak to Chelsea again and make sure she was ready to do whatever it took to get out of here once and for all.

"Fine. We will do that. You won't have much time, though. We need to talk to your dad first," Ames said, and beckoned me to stand near a computer on the far edge of the wall.

"None of us have cell phones or wristlets that can communicate with the outside world," Jacob explained, as he booted up the computer. "But I've developed a tool to make a call to someone using this device. I've tested it out as anonymous calls to the outside—to random places—to make sure it's a good connection."

"But what do people see when you call? What about caller ID?"

"There is no phone number calling from this machine—"

"Will my dad be able to tell where we are? What can I tell him about our location?"

"We're not sure, exactly. All we know is that we're somewhere in the Indian Ocean—a place away from shipping channels, in an area most humans will never pass."

"And how come no one has ever come across us before? Isn't someone looking for all of the kids that go missing?" I asked.

"No," Ames said. "No one is looking for anyone here. Every prisoner here is presumed dead under other circumstances."

And something else was bothering me too. "What about satellite imagery? Don't maps show that this island exists?"

"No, they do not, unfortunately. That was very important to Gareth. Bertram actually helped Gareth with that technology way back when he first chose this island as our future home," Ames said. "Gareth described this place as a Utopia that people would try to ruin if they knew about it. He needed Bertram's help hiding it from the world—making it invisible. Bertram had no idea what he was really doing, helping Gareth conceal the Island for its evil purposes."

"So you really don't know where we are?"

"We don't know the exact latitude and longitude, just the approximate region. On a map, we just appear as ocean—nothing else. It's like we don't exist," Jacob explained, his face getting redder by the minute.

"And no one has ever accidentally happened upon us?"

"No. Gareth has boats stationed out at sea— pirates—to ensure if anyone even comes close, they are redirected—" Jacob said.

"How are they redirected?"

"Through intimidation or force, if necessary. They don't know what they're defending exactly, or who's responsible—just that ridiculous amounts of money appear in their offshore bank accounts every week as long as they're stationed out there."

"And why doesn't anyone come down to try to stop them? Isn't that suspicious?" I asked.

"Reed, if you could watch the news, you'd see there are a lot bigger problems going on in the world than some pirates in the Indian Ocean," Ames said.

"What do you mean?"

"I mean no one is going to spend time and money trying to stop some pirates from a territorial pissing contest in an area of the ocean that's not a shipping route. Make sense?"

"I don't know—" I was trying to make sense of everything. "So, what do I tell my dad?" I asked.

"Tell him everything—that you're alive. And that Gareth is still alive too. That he faked his plane death years ago and that he's been holding you and many others hostage on an island," Ames continued. "It will sound outlandish, we realize. But if your dad hears your voice, he will know it's you."

"Tell him our approximate location—that we are outside of shipping routes, and tell him about Praeclarus, but don't name any names. If it leaks to any of them that your dad knows about what is happening here, then everything will be over. They all have a way to communicate to Gareth immediately," Jacob warned.

"Okay, I understand. But what if he doesn't believe me? It's such a crazy story."

It sounded too bizarre even hearing Ames talk through it out loud. I didn't know if my dad would ever believe me, except why would I make something like that up?

I felt myself getting emotional, thinking about making contact with the outside world after so long. It was the first step to saving myself and others from being killed on the Island.

I envisioned getting on a boat again, heading away from the Island and how amazing that would be to leave all of this behind once and for all, hopefully with Chelsea, Delphine, Micah and Ames by my side, alive. They had each helped me get through this, and I would help them too.

I vowed that when we got home, we'd figure out a way to make sure everyone was safe and protected from the wrath of any Praeclarus members who weren't jailed immediately when we were out in the world. We'd have to figure out how to protect all of us—for the rest of our lives. I was sure Gareth's network could get to us at any point, forever. It was a scary thought, but better than the alternative of dying here.

I wanted to talk to my mom too, but Ames and Jacob told me not to ask for her, as my dad would have to handle everything without alerting too many people—just his own security teams, as necessary. There was too much of a risk of the story getting out before they reached us if several people knew.

We'd maybe need to go into hiding for a while—for who knew how long—away from our house, away from Oregon. But where would we go? That would have to be figured out later.

"Okay, well, no time like the present. Let's do this," Jacob said as he tapped the screen numerous times, bringing up new commands and long lines of code. I wasn't sure what was happening until I heard a dial tone.

"What's your dad's number? Come enter it," Ames said. My dad had several phones and wristlets that he used for calls, but he had a special line dedicated just to family. Only a few people knew that number—my mom, me, my grandparents, and my dad's siblings—I think that was it—so if he saw a call coming through that line, he knew to answer it.

I punched in the number. The line rang and my heart felt like it was going to burst right out of my chest as we waited for my dad to pick up. One ring. Two ring. Three rings. Nothing. Where was he? He always answered this phone. It kept on ringing and ringing and ringing, but didn't go to voicemail. My dad didn't believe in voicemail.

"I can't believe he isn't answering," I said. Maybe he was in a meeting. We'd have to try again, but when? I tried not to feel the crushing sense of disappointment as it continued to ring, filling the whole room.

Lionel was snickering at the back of the room. I felt devastated. I'd even settle for a voicemail greeting, or anything at all. Any sign of my dad.

"Hmm . . . " Jacob said, thinking. "Well, there's one other option—let's send him a message."

"What do you mean? How?"

"We can take a video of you and send it to him—a canned version is not as good as a live conversation, but it will have to do."

"Okay," I said, agreeing that it was a good option, considering. "But we will need to talk to him at some point, to confirm that he's coming to help."

"Yes, we will break you out—"

RINNNNNNNNNNNNNNNNNNNNNNNNG!
RINNNNNNNNG! A loud bell started to sound.
Jacob jumped up and ran over to a monitor on the left side of the room.

"What is that?" I yelled over the deafening sound. Ames looked at Jacob who was staring at one screen, like he saw a ghost.

"Reed, you need to get out of here now and get back to your living quarters. There's a Suit waiting for you there, just in case. You understand me?" Ames barked, pushing me toward the door.

"What? What do you mean? What's going on?"

"I programmed that alarm in this security room to alert us when Gareth leaves his quarters between eleven p.m. and five a.m. It's the middle of the night. This is highly unusual," Jacob said.

"What about you? And him?" I asked, trying to

understand, pointing toward Lionel, and then at Jacob.

"Don't worry about us. We need to separate now. You're going to have to find your way back on your own—" Ames said, as he pushed me out the door.

"And what about my dad?" I asked, but before I could say another word, Ames slammed the door.

I turned to face the path and looked out at the murky darkness. The tree cover in this area was so heavy, it was nearly impossible to see anything at all. I could barely even spot my own hand in front of my face.

I knew I didn't have a choice and I'd have to find my way back on my own. I tried to remember which path we took to get to the security building. I started down the hill, tripping over rocks and roots and branches as I ran as fast as I could go. Ames had assured me earlier that any Suits we'd encounter would be on our side, unless Gareth had sent out a new set of people or we ran into traitors, like Lionel. We didn't know why Gareth was up or where he was going at three in the morning.

I stumbled a few times, falling on my face and getting up as quickly as I could, ignoring the pain as I felt blood drip down from my scraped knees to my ankles and into my shoe bed.

I got to the first fork in the road and thought back to the way we came and went left. The trees overhead started to thin out a little bit. I continued to run quickly, not stopping to wonder if anyone was hiding in the shadows, watching me.

I'd have to hurry to avoid Gareth. If he went to our living quarters and I wasn't there, it would be a huge problem. I finally got to a clearing where I could see the buildings down below and I saw the bunker that held our cells. I ran there, quickly glancing to both sides to see if anyone else was around. No one was in sight, and I finally got to the door and looked to the right and to the left. I would need someone to let me in.

Suddenly, the door opened and there was Trevor, my fellow Ship Out mate, in his white suit.

"Don't worry, I'm here to help you. We haven't seen Gareth yet, you're lucky."

"Phew," I said quietly and stepped in and he quickly shut the door behind me.

"Now, let's go," he said, ushering me down the hall. "And be quiet. Everyone is still asleep."

I was silent and incredibly grateful for Trevor's help. We finally got to the door and he entered the code. He took me to my cell door, opened and closed it ever-so quietly, and I lay down on my bed. I looked at Trevor, smiling appreciatively. He nodded his head like he understood, then he was out the door and gone.

I got up, went to my sink, and put a cloth in water and dabbed my bloody knees. I then changed my clothes back into pajamas and lay down, surprised to feel like I could fall asleep immediately.

CHAPTER 16

The next day, I got up quickly, anxious to confirm that Ames was back in the training area and that Gareth hadn't caught him.

I got up, put on my training gear, brushed my teeth, and looked in the mirror. I was very tan and more muscular than I'd ever been during my years of wrestling. I'd probably gained twenty pounds of muscle since being here, with our large meals and constant workouts. As I stared at myself, I realized that I was a completely different person than I'd been prior to coming to the island. No longer an addict, but now strong—a physical force, completely in control of my body and mind.

It was a new sensation—I'd been addicted and had a drink or a toke or a line on a daily basis for two years. I'd given up wrestling to feed my addiction and to hang out with my friends—the friends my parents didn't like and said were a bad influence on me. I always knew it was the other way around. *I* was the bad influence, egging on my friends to take a hit, or chug the beer, or steal the vodka from the store. I'd been such a shithead and gotten away from who I really was—from the person my parents raised me to be.

As I looked in the mirror, I saw that person again—finally—after he'd been hidden away for so long. It was just the violence in me that I'd need to kill now. It was a strange sensation, being free in one regard, but stuck in a place where I might die unless I used violence to secure my survival. It felt unjust, being a seventeen-year-old kid forced into this situation.

I thought about all the things I still wanted to do with my life. I wanted to go to Barcelona and

see all the weird buildings. I wanted to learn how to fly a plane—that sounded cool. I wanted to take a girl on a proper date, like out to dinner and then go for a walk and hold hands and fool around while I was sober. I'd kissed Chelsea, and I wanted it to be her. She was the person I imagined by my side once we got out of here.

I needed to try to call my dad again. Now that Elise was dead and Chelsea was locked up, I depended on Ames and Jacob to get me that opportunity.

The Suits escorted us to breakfast, and I snuck a peek at their faces, trying to figure out who was on our side. A Suit who'd never made eye contact with me before caught my glance and nodded with just a slight smile, as if sending me a sign. I wondered if he was on my side or not, otherwise that seemed like an odd gesture.

We got to the dining hall, with its walls lined with pictures of our fights—like sports photography, but with kids stabbing each other and grappling, and Suits holding up arms of victors. There were a few pictures of me, mid-battle, with a crazed look in my eye, like I was someone else—a person I didn't even recognize. I didn't like that version of me—the killer, the guy who got wrapped up in the moment mid-battle and would do anything to win and survive.

I sat down at the end of the table, my usual spot, away from everyone else, and Delphine and Micah settled in across from me.

"You look exhausted, Reed," she said, raising her eyebrows and looking at me with that mischievous expression. "What sort of trouble have you been getting into?"

"What do you mean?" I probably sounded more defensive than I meant to, but I remembered what Ames said about not saying anything to anyone at any cost. I needed to trust him and keep my mouth shut, even if it was hard.

"Well, what happened to your knees?" she

asked, poking her head down to stare at my legs. Micah followed suit.

"Woah, dude. When did that happen?"

I tried to think quickly but really no good reason came to me. "It happened during training yesterday, when we were grappling. Don't you remember?"

"Uh . . . no . . . I don't remember that at all," Delphine said, lowering her voice. "Is something going on, and you're not telling us?"

"No. Why would you even think that?" I asked. Delphine and I had always been an open book to each other so I wasn't sure why she was so persistent right now. I wondered if she didn't trust me. "I'm still waiting for the go-ahead from Ames."

Perfectly timed, the Suits brought over plates of waffles, topped with fresh, sliced strawberries and sides of crispy bacon. I changed the subject, talking about how hungry I was and that I couldn't wait to eat and get back out there today.

After the meal, we got up and headed out to the training floor, and I was relieved to see Ames standing there. He was the only instructor out in the field. He didn't look over at me when we entered, but ordered the group to gather around him.

We all jogged over to him.

"Sit down for a moment," he instructed and we got down on the ground.

Delphine was next to me. I glanced at her and she leaned her head on my shoulder. She smelled sweet, and her soft hair tickled my shoulder. I felt myself blushing.

Ames stood over us, looking down. His face was still very swollen and discolored but I didn't see any signs of new injuries, which made me think that Gareth hadn't caught him while out and about last night.

"So, friends, as you know, the Praeclarus members will start arriving in a few days, which also means that a few of you are going to be dead within the week—I'd say at least five of you—and then maybe soon, we'll be joined by new kids to replace the ones that were killed in battle. You are all replaceable. How does that make you feel?"

"Angry," I called out. "Pissed off."

I knew what Ames was trying to do, to rally these kids to fight with us, not against us, when the time came. We'd need all of them on our side when the time was right.

"It's not fair that we were brought here—brought here to die. Gareth thought so little of each of us—that we were druggies, gang members, assholes or whatever—he's using us for pawns in his game. So when it's your time to fight in the ring, you have to step it up and bring your best to live to fight another day," I said.

"What are you saying?" Delphine asked Ames, taking her head from my shoulder and furrowing her brow, confused. "I thought you were on Gareth's side?"

"I am, but I'm here to make sure you each

succeed to the best of your abilities, whatever you face," Ames said. "It will make for better battles, and each of you has to be even tougher now that there are the Creatures involved, right?"

Everyone agreed, and he then directed us to start our warm-up exercise. He wouldn't catch my eye each time I would run by and I guessed we had to be even more careful now. I didn't know what happened last night and I was dying for the opportunity to reach out to my dad again.

Mid-training I noticed Gareth walk in and sit down to watch us.

"Delphine," he called to her, and she cringed at the sound of his voice. She slowly walked over to him and he put his arm around her waist and pulled her down onto his lap. He whispered something in her ear that I couldn't hear and she seemed disturbed.

"I have to go now," Delphine said to Ames, and she and Gareth got up to leave.

"Where are you taking her?" I yelled after them

and Delphine turned back, staring at me with a pleading gaze as if there was anything I could do to help.

Micah appeared crestfallen but there was nothing either of us could do to help her.

CHAPTER 17

Later in the day's training, I went to go get a drink, then sat in the tiny sliver of shade along the wall. Ames came over to me.

"Do you trust Delphine completely?" he asked. It was the first thing that came out of his mouth toward me all day. Nothing about what transpired last night. Nothing about contacting my dad again or where Gareth had gone overnight. I was dying to know.

"What do you mean?" I asked, caught off-guard by the question. "Of course I trust her. Why wouldn't I?"

He turned to see who was watching and I

saw Micah staring at us, but out of earshot. This conversation was taking an unexpected turn.

"Something is off about her, isn't it?"

I did think she was strange, it was true, but nothing malicious. She just seemed eager to get on with the plan to get out of here, but who wasn't?

"What do you mean? I'm not following."

"Well, I've trained a lot of kids in my day—athletes and non-athletes alike—and she always seemed better at everything than she was letting on. She's very good—better than you, even, if she was given the chance to really fight you."

"Hey—" I said, trying not to feel offended by that. *Was it really true? Maybe.*

"Well, maybe she's just a quick learner," I said, not following his train of thought.

"And there's something else—"

"What is it?"

"In all of my time on the Island, I've never seen Gareth take someone back to his room so many times. It's very unusual."

"So? Maybe he really likes her—or maybe she does something—" I stopped, feeling gross for even talking about it. I didn't like thinking about Gareth and Delphine together.

"I've just never seen that—he's a very particular man. He moves on immediately."

"Okay, well Delphine is different, we all know that. She's cute, she's funny, everyone loves her— I'm sure Gareth just likes spending time with her."

"Well, I'd just keep her at arm's length if I were you. Something doesn't add up right. And Micah too—they have a thing, don't they?"

I shrugged. I honestly wasn't sure what went on between them—there was no real opportunity for them to be together here without someone helping them. I'd never seen them kiss, just little affection-ate touches and lots of hushed conversations that would stop when I walked up. They always played it off like a joke, but I did suspect that they were together and hiding it from me.

I realized that maybe they had had something

on the boat—it would've been possible there. I remembered Micah leaving our room a few times in the middle of the night. When I had asked him about it, he said he needed fresh air. But now the more I thought about it, I bet he was sneaking off to be with Delphine. *It makes sense.*

"So Gareth didn't catch anyone last night?"

"No, but we can't talk about that now. We have to get back to training, don't we? Jacob is sorting everything out, don't you worry."

"How could I not?" I asked as we walked back to where Micah was stretching.

"Everything all right, man?"

"Yeah, I'm just anxious to get the ball rolling," I said. I considered saying more, or asking him something about Delphine.

"How does Delphine remain so strong when she has to go be with Gareth?" I finally asked.

"She's one tough girl, isn't she? I've never met anyone anyone quite like her. And I bet you feel the same way, huh?" he asked.

"I like her, but not like that," I responded.

"C'mon, man, you can tell me. You think she's cute, don't you?" Micah asked.

"Yeah. That goes without saying. Hey Micah— tell me the truth. You guys are together, aren't you? Why are you hiding it from me?"

"What? No! Why do you ask?" he answered quickly, sounding defensive.

"I don't know, man. You guys just seem like you are always in on a secret, and I'm on the outside looking in at you."

"What does that mean? Really?" he asked, narrowing his gaze at me.

He sounded annoyed now, which was weird for Micah. He'd never been short with me before.

"I don't know—I just assumed you had coupled up."

"No man, not at all. You're funny, you know that?" he asked, the good-natured lift in his voice returning again. He got up then and went to the fountain to get a sip of water.

I couldn't figure out what was wrong with him, but I was sure that he and Delphine were together. So why were they trying to hide it?

CHAPTER 18

Delphine came back later that afternoon. Everyone stopped and turned to stare at her as she entered. She put on a brave face, smiling at us, and I wondered what she had been doing with Gareth.

It was true that Gareth had taken a special interest in her—that he liked to take her away to spend time with him, and that she seemed less disturbed by it than she should. But I chalked that up to her being a tough girl who didn't want to show any weakness.

She trotted over to us and gave Micah a long hug and then turned to me.

"We need to escalate the plan and right

away. You're going to be facing a Creature, Reed, in the next battle. Gareth told me it will be you."

"Why would he tell you that?" I asked, digging in a little bit. I saw Ames standing just a few feet behind us, watching us talk.

"Why wouldn't he? He knows how close we are and I'm sure he's just trying to psyche you out. He's pretty good at that," she said.

"What sort of Creature will it be?" I asked, trying to see how much she knew.

"That I don't know—" she said, sounding dismissive.

"I've been thinking about all the Praeclarus members and who they are. I wonder why they're so loyal to Gareth and why none of them have ever spoken a word about what happens here."

"Yeah?" Delphine leaned in. "So, what's your point?"

"Nothing. I just find it strange, that's all."

I was disturbed by Ames's accusation that something was off about Delphine. She was standing in front of me now, smiling, but she had just spent several hours with Gareth and seemed totally fine.

He had put her up in battle though—would he do that to someone who had ulterior motives? It didn't seem likely to me and I tried to figure out what could possibly be Delphine's angle. She hated this place just as much as I did. And we had talked many times about what we'd do when we got out.

I decided that Ames was just being cautious. He came over finally and said that it was time to go inside for the day and that we were finishing early—Gareth's orders.

"What's happening?" Delphine asked as we walked inside, appearing genuinely confused. We were standing directly behind Ames, who turned to us.

"Gareth is treating you to a special dinner. He'll be the guest of honor, of course—and all of you guys will be too," he said.

"Why?" I asked.

"I don't know. He didn't tell me. But you get

to go the Praeclarus dining hall—so it's an extra-special meal. You all need to shower and then we'll take you there."

It felt like something bigger was at play than a simple dinner.

"Do you know what's going on?" I asked Delphine as we walked back to our cell building.

She shook her head. "No, I don't—Gareth didn't say anything about a dinner," she said and once we got into our living quarters, she headed to the girls' shower and we headed to the boys' one.

"What do you think is going on?" I asked Micah.

"Probably some elaborate scheme to make us more miserable," he guessed.

We washed up and got dressed in our civilian clothes—or as Gareth called them, our non-training gear. I wore a pair of jeans and a gray t-shirt—the standard attire for all of us when we weren't going to work out.

The Suits came to escort us to the dining hall.

We were led down the marble outdoor corridor. I'm sure it was the same path that Elise led me down so many nights ago, blindfolded, when she was still alive.

This is where the Praeclarus members mingled when they first arrived. This is where they walked freely, no fear for their own life or safety. This is where they laughed and drank while the prisoners toiled away in training, getting ready to entertain them, to be on the other side of a wager for money.

We entered the grand dining hall and it was huge, with dark wood columns and high ceilings. The front wall was lined with the heads of different exotic animals, stuffed, with eyes replaced by glassy marble-like orbs. There were two tigers, a lion with a huge golden mane, a rhinoceros, a grizzly bear, and many smaller animals whose mouths were open, exposing sharpened teeth and an expression of terror captured forever.

As we gathered around the animals, I went to

look at the gold plaques listing which Praeclarus members had killed each one. I stared at every plaque, trying to re-memorize each name. I wanted to have a list of everyone who was part of this place to make sure they were accounted for and punished after we got back.

Gareth walked through the door, flanked by many Suits. He was wearing a linen outfit—cream and grey, with purple accents on his lapel. He was very tan and looked well rested and comfortable, not like a man becoming more and more paranoid every day.

"Everyone, please take a seat," he instructed, and I saw that the long wooden table had enough chairs for all of us to sit, even the Suits, which was unusual. Would they be joining us?

Gareth recognized everyone's momentary hesitation. "Yes, even my Suits, please sit down. I want us all to enjoy a meal together. I feel like there's a divide between us and I've heard rumblings that some of you are thinking about rising up against me."

He didn't look at me specifically, but scanned the room, taking everything in. I momentarily thought that maybe Delphine had said something to him—and then I felt bad that I had that notion, even for just a moment. I didn't understand why Ames was trying to turn me against her, to make me question her intentions.

She was sitting right next to me, and underneath the table, she reached over and grabbed my hand, squeezing it tightly.

I looked over at her and smiled. It was like she could read my mind and she was trying to reassure me.

"I want us all to sit down together and get to know each other. And at the end of the evening, I'm going to let one of you go free, no strings attached."

The crowd erupted in murmured conversations of disbelief.

"Really?" this kid named Drake asked.

Gareth turned toward him. "Yes, really. I just want to hear your stories on why you think you should go and I'll pick the most worthy person to get on a helicopter tonight to say goodbye to all of this—" he said, as he looked around the grand building. Then, with a snap, he ushered in the Suits to bring a plate of food to each of us. Then they sat down as well.

"Why are you doing this?" I asked him, feeling skeptical and certain this was some sort of trick.

"I want to show all of you that there's still just a little heart left in me. Just a sliver, really."

It didn't make sense to me, but everyone else started cautiously talking to each other as they began to eat their food. I took a few bites but my appetite disappeared and I mostly moved my food around on my plate.

"So, before we begin, who'd want this ticket off the Island tonight, if I gave it to you?" he asked, looking down the table at everyone. There were about fifty of us sitting here, and no one raised his or her hand at first. I imagined everyone was scared, like this was some sort of trap.

"Well, if you're not honest with me, it'll be a real shame. I only want to give this opportunity to someone who really wants it—who feels like they've learned a good lesson during their time here. A person who will promise me that they'll be a better member of society when they return. So, anyone? Anyone going to volunteer that they'd be interested in this offer?"

I wanted to see where he was going with this, so I raised my hand. Slowly a few others followed suit. Delphine raised her hand, and Micah. Gareth looked around the room down each side of the table, like he was memorizing what he was seeing.

"And which of you think you have a better life here on the Island than you'd ever have at home?"

There was a long pause and I saw five kids that I'd fought with raise their hands—all poseurs, idiots—and several Suits.

"That certainly was very interesting. You five—" he said, pointing to the kids with their arms raised, "you are becoming Suits tonight. No more fighting for you."

Everyone else around me groaned, but the five boys clapped excitedly, and didn't seem to mind one bit that they were leaving the fighting behind and joining a life of a different kind of servitude.

"And the person I pick to go home tonight is . . . hmm . . . this is a tough one. I think I'm going to go with my gut, based on what I've seen tonight and your general behavior since coming to the Island. Let's see—who should I pick?"

A few people called out "Me! Me!" but I remained quiet, not believing for an instant that this wasn't a trick.

"Micah—it'll be you," Gareth said abruptly, like he landed on a decision all at once.

"Me?" Micah asked, sounding incredulous. "Why me?" he asked, and I could feel many sets

of jealous eyes on Micah, who seemed utterly confused.

"Not Micah, please!" Delphine called out and
Micah shot her a look.

"I chose Micah because he doesn't complain
and he just gets his work done. He's a leader who
engenders people's trust. I think he is staged to do
bigger and better things with his life," Gareth said,
and Micah looked embarrassed by the attention.
"So, I'm going to let him go tonight—"

"Why are you doing this, Gareth?" Ames asked,
with concern in his voice.

"Well, I'm actually here to make you all a deal.
I've heard of a great unrest—that there are people
among you that are setting up a coup to try to take
me out. But if that happens, I don't know which
of you I'll be able to protect and I may just need
to take everyone out at once. I'm a proud man and
I won't go to jail, so if I need to blow this whole
place out of the water at once, I will—"

He was trying to scare us, to get people on his

side again before the revolt started, to strike fear in everyone, to get them to turn on us when we tried to rally them to our side. I saw what he was doing and I'm sure Ames saw through it as well, but everyone else was listening intently.

"So, that being said, if you hear anything—anything at all about who is behind all the planning and when it's going to happen, come to me and I will reward you handsomely. I will let you out of here, just like Micah."

"Micah, come here," Gareth said and Micah got up and headed to where Gareth was now standing, staring out a large floor-to-ceiling window that opened out toward a bluff above the ocean.

I turned to look and I saw a helicopter landing there. It was the first one I'd seen since coming to the Island.

"See that, Micah? That's your ticket out of here. And please, also take this," he said, handing over a large black briefcase. "Go ahead, open it."

Micah knelt to the ground and flipped the

latches on the case. Inside of it were stacks of money.

"That's for you to create a new life, or to return to the life that you had. Your choice, but it will enable you to not only survive, but thrive."

"I don't know what to say," Micah said. "Can I please take them with me?" Micah asked, pointing toward Delphine and me. Delphine looked distraught, and I couldn't believe that Micah was about to leave us, unless this was a trick too.

"No, I'm afraid not," Gareth said. Micah was upset but I knew he really had no choice. He had to take the offer.

"Okay," he said and he walked over and gave me a hug, and then gave Delphine a very, very long embrace and whispered something in her ear.

She smiled ever so slightly, and a single, fat tear rolled down her cheek.

A few new Suits came up and led Micah away.

We finished eating in silence, but there was a different energy in the room—like there was possibly a way out of here that didn't involve fighting to the death.

In the distance, I saw the helicopter take off and fly out of sight, and it all felt very grim.

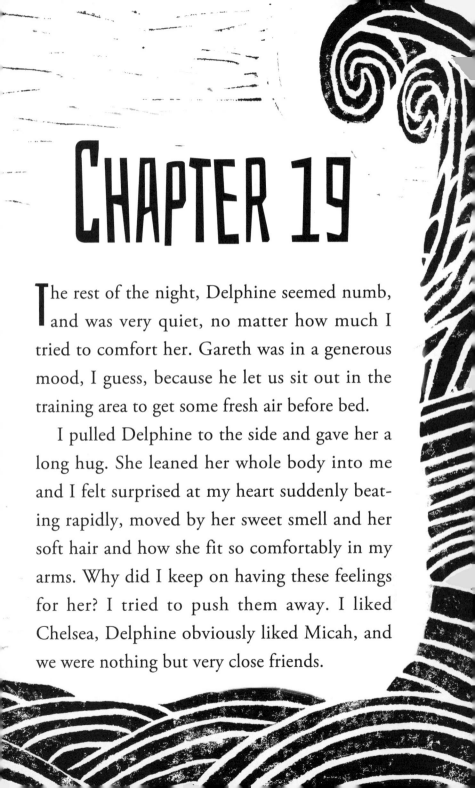

CHAPTER 19

The rest of the night, Delphine seemed numb, and was very quiet, no matter how much I tried to comfort her. Gareth was in a generous mood, I guess, because he let us sit out in the training area to get some fresh air before bed.

I pulled Delphine to the side and gave her a long hug. She leaned her whole body into me and I felt surprised at my heart suddenly beating rapidly, moved by her sweet smell and her soft hair and how she fit so comfortably in my arms. Why did I keep on having these feelings for her? I tried to push them away. I liked Chelsea, Delphine obviously liked Micah, and we were nothing but very close friends.

"Where do you think he'll go? Back home?" she asked.

"I'm not sure."

I had no idea at all, and I felt like it wasn't the end of the story. My gut was that we'd hear from Micah again.

It was very dark. We lay on the ground next to each other, and we stared up at the stars. Everyone else was scattered around the field. The whole sky was filled, like someone had thrown a giant handful of stars against the sky to see what would stick. Many of them shot across the sky. Every time someone saw one they'd yell out and it seemed like everyone else was in a good mood. I think everyone was happy that Gareth had given us a little bit more room to enjoy ourselves for just one evening.

Delphine turned over on her side, facing me, and I turned toward her and put my arms around her to hug her again. Our faces brushed up against each other and I don't know what came over me but suddenly I found myself kissing her. She kissed me back, and it was a surprise, especially since I thought I liked Chelsea. And yet, Delphine had a weird hold over me. I found her to be exotic and strange and funny and bossy, and I liked the combination of all of those things.

Our kiss was more amazing than I expected it to be and I felt a jolt run through me. I pulled away and quickly glanced around to see if anyone noticed us, but we were far enough away and it was very dark.

"Do it again," Delphine said, and I wrapped my fingers through her hair and pulled her in again for a longer, harder kiss. It felt like the ground beneath us was falling away, and my heart got all confused, because it seemed familiar somehow, like we'd done this before.

What the hell am I doing? I asked myself. I was pretty sure this was foolish, but then I wondered if I was just testing her in some subconscious way, to see if she felt like she was really on my side. It felt real, the kiss, and the way she kissed me back.

I was alarmed that I'd made a big mistake, complicating everything further.

"Oh, Reed . . . what are we doing?" she asked and I couldn't help but laugh a little bit. I was feeling the same way. "I think I might just be mourning Micah being gone . . . " she said finally, and then her voice trailed off.

We sat there quietly; I was unsure what to say.

"Do you think we're ever going to get out of here?" Delphine finally asked. I wasn't sure, of course, but it felt possible for the first time.

"I think so. We tried to contact my dad the other night," I said, just blurting it out. I felt a great relief not having this hidden between us any longer. I was not meant to keep secrets—not while sober, at least—when my head and brain were clear.

"What do you mean?" she asked, sitting up suddenly. "Why didn't you tell me this before?"

She looked genuinely upset and I felt badly that I'd kept it from her. She'd been my best friend through this whole process, and doubts had turned me against her.

"I wasn't sure I could trust you. We were wondering why you were spending so much time alone with Gareth," I said and her face darkened.

"Who's we? You mean Ames?" she asked. I didn't want to throw him under the bus, so I didn't say anything. We were quiet and I knew she was annoyed.

"Well—what happened when you contacted him?" she asked, looking at me expectantly. "You left out the most important part."

"He didn't pick up his phone, so I don't know. We let it ring and ring and ring, and nothing happened. It's a private line just for family. He always picks up. It was strange, but I think that he was at a business meeting or something. We're going to try again really soon."

"That's awful," Delphine said. "So, when are you going to take another shot at it?"

I shrugged. I honestly didn't know.

"And who else was helping you?" she asked. The question gave me pause for just a moment, like she was trying to extract information from me that she didn't need if she was on my side.

"Just Ames, actually," I said, remembering what Ames said about Jacob, and that no one could know about Jacob's involvement. There were many layers of deceit all around us and I didn't know why I still felt compelled to keep this from her.

She looked relieved and we heard the Suits call us over to head back inside. She leaned in and kissed me one last time, like she couldn't help herself.

"I'm so glad to hear that everything is in motion—please don't keep me in the dark any longer. I need to know what's going on so I can protect you when Gareth asks for me," she said, and that did seem logical.

As we were walking indoors, one of the Suits grabbed Delphine. "You're heading with me.

Gareth's asking for you again. I'd love to know what makes you so special," he said, looking her up and down like she was a piece of meat.

"I bet you do," she said and wriggled out of his grip. She gave me one last look goodbye before going down a separate hallway away from us.

I went back to my room and couldn't sleep, thinking about Micah and where he was and if Gareth had been telling the truth. I wondered if Micah would try to alert someone and save us. But again, that didn't seem likely to me, given Gareth's need to protect the Island.

Was Micah taken somewhere to be killed, or used in Gareth's game in some other way? I hoped Delphine would find out more from Gareth tonight.

I thought about kissing Delphine. The feeling jarred me, like we'd done it before. She was so comfortable and natural. And there was Chelsea, too. Was she still in her same isolation cell? I wanted to talk to her, but now I felt guilty, like I'd betrayed her by kissing Delphine. It was foolish. We weren't dating—this wasn't real life.

When Jacob came to get me again, I'd insist we needed to see her. I wanted to make sure she was okay and that she was still alive. I was surprised Gareth was punishing her for this long—his own daughter. But why was I surprised, really? This was a guy who killed his daughter's mother and his best friend, and spent years engineering monsters to fight kids to the death.

I tossed and turned, knowing Praeclarus members would be arriving in a few days and it would be too late to avoid getting them into this mess.

And now, with Gareth's promise that he'd let people leave if they reported any revolt plans, we had to be even more careful about how to move the plans forward with everyone else. We weren't sure who'd side with us and who'd quickly rat us out.

I was bothered by the fact that the hangar where the Creatures were housed was run by a different security system than the one Jacob managed. Who made sure those animals stayed inside—and couldn't they let them out if Gareth ordered it?

Everyone around me was still awake, but it was odd that Micah's voice wasn't one of the people who was cracking jokes and talking about what happened. He'd be excited by these developments, although I'm sure he'd be angry with me for kissing Delphine, even if he didn't come out and say it.

Was he on his way to a different life—a better life somewhere—or was he still trapped on the Island? Maybe he'd been put in solitary confinement. I was sure there was a bigger agenda for Micah and that picking him wasn't just arbitrary.

I waited to hear from Ames or Jacob but neither of them came and I eventually fell asleep, exhausted from another weird day.

When I woke up the next morning, I was surprised to see that Ames was standing just outside my cell. I stood up and approached the bars so we could talk quietly.

"I heard a rumor that the Praeclarus boats are coming in early . . . before Saturday," he said.

"What? Why?"

"I'm not sure, but I think they'll be here sooner than we had hoped."

"So, what about the plan?" I whispered.

"It's still happening, it will just be more dramatic than before. You remember where to go?"

"Yes, I think so," I said, recalling where Jacob's bunker was in my mind.

"Just be ready to move. You'll know when the time comes, trust me."

"Okay," I said. I knew he was taking a big risk standing here talking to me like this, out in the open.

I put on my most comfortable training shorts and a t-shirt, and my sneakers.

"Good. See you on the other side," he said, before walking past the cell areas and saying hello to everyone else as they awakened, as if it was a normal day.

No one seemed the wiser and everyone got ready like normal. I brushed my teeth and stared at myself in the mirror, trying to psyche myself up for what I was going to have to do today.

This time I'd reach my dad. I'd tell him everything and I'd figure out with him how to piece together where we were located. We'd save us all.

This is what Ames had been training me for—for a day like today. This was my real test. I could feel it, and I was ready to face whatever the day would bring.

We were called to the dining hall and I stayed toward the back as we left, anxious for the war plan to be set in motion.

CHAPTER 20

As we filed into the dining hall, it seemed like a normal day on the surface. Everyone was joking around with each other, but there was a level of tension in the air as Gareth had announced to everyone that Praeclarus was coming in earlier than Saturday, and everybody had to push up the preparation schedule to get the Island ready.

The female and male companions—as Gareth called them—were all at the Island's spa, getting cleaned and primped and ready to celebrate a new vacation week with their Praeclarus counterparts. Some of them had had the same partner for many trips, whereas other Praeclarus members liked to mix things up and choose someone new each time—a blonde one trip and then a redhead the next, a woman one day and a man the next.

We were told that many of the Suits were outside getting the island ready for the Praeclarus members' arrival—it was always a very busy week when they were on their way. There were Suits assigned to power-washing the docks, and others that were readying the guest quarters or prepping a week of extravagant feasts. There were some that were in the game area, cleaning up the shit and feeding the animals, and others who were sweeping the Coliseum. A few were testing the fighters' microphones. It was a mini society, each person with a unique job, and everyone had their place.

As we entered the dining room, I looked around and saw that we were only accompanied by three Suits versus the normal six, and that we already had food at each place setting—a large bowl of cereal with a small jar of milk. Of course, the chefs

were too busy getting the meals ready for a week of debauchery to make anything extravagant for us. There was no Max or Darby or Titus or Gareth, either. There was a false sense of calmness, like this was just a normal day.

Everyone took their seats and started eating. Delphine was glum and not her usual self. I wanted to comfort her but I knew this was not the time or place to do it.

As we were eating, suddenly the door on the far end of the room swung open and four people stormed in. They were big men dressed in all black, with their faces concealed by masks. They were each holding a large machine gun and they pushed their way inside.

"Get down! Get down!" they yelled.

"What's going on here?" one of the Suits yelled, barging toward the shortest masked man holding the gun. The Suit had his zapper, but that was it. He stuck it outward like he was going to incapacitate the man, but the intruder didn't hesitate for a moment.

Bang!

He shot the Suit dead, the Suit crumpling to the ground in a lump, blood pouring out of him onto the cement.

We all scrambled to the floor and put our faces down against the ground. I tried to peek up and see what they were doing, but one of the men came over quickly, stomping in big black boots.

"Put your head down now!" he yelled. I was too far away to comfort Delphine, who was across the table, on the other side of its legs.

The room was still except for the violent movements of the men wearing black, and we could hear them whispering to each other.

Suddenly, I felt a hand on my back and it pulled me up almost silently. I looked at the person, and through the mask's eyeholes, I recognized Ames's stare.

He didn't say anything but pushed me toward

the door, his heavy footsteps echoing in my ear. I knew not to dare to speak, and when we got to the door, he pushed me out and shut it behind him to deal with the dining hall himself.

I glanced up at the cameras mounted on the ceiling and I assumed that they had been altered so no one was watching me, or at least no one who also didn't want to get out of here. I didn't see any other Suits within immediate sight, and I knew what I needed to do.

Run.

Without a second thought, I bolted down the hallway toward the outdoors. I burst through the doors and was immediately blinded by the sunlight. My eyes took a second to adjust, and I looked over and saw a Suit staring at me.

He looked like he'd seen a ghost and I wondered if he was about to alert someone. Should I just take him out here and now, and not give him the chance?

"So—" he finally said. "It's really happening?"

He sounded hopeful. "You better get going now, before someone else comes."

I turned and without a second thought, started running up the path that led to the mountain, which looked completely different in daylight.

"Good luck!" I heard him yell after me. I didn't take a moment longer to respond.

CHAPTER 21

The path was very narrow, constructed from packed dirt and rocks and gnarled tree roots. The vegetation on the side was very thick. There was no one else around. I took the first fork in the road and suddenly, I came upon another Suit that was clearing old branches and leaves from the path.

"Hey! What are you doing up here?" he asked, looking at me, and reached in his pocket for something.

Without a second thought, I charged him and tackled him, his head hitting against the ground with a loud smack. He swung out his arms as if trying to stop me, and I took a rock that was next to his body and brought it down hard against the side of his head, knocking him out.

I pulled his dead weight into the bushes quickly and tried to obstruct him from view of anyone passing by, although he was wearing a white suit, so it was impossible to hide him completely.

There was also a spot of wet blood now on the path, so I hoped there would not be many more visitors. I'd have to move very quickly.

I kept on running, hitting many forks in the road, retracing my steps from the other night.

I heard something in the distance—someone yelling out—and I stopped for a moment straining to hear what it was.

"You . . . can't . . . keep . . . me . . . here . . . forever! Help me!" The person yelled, and it was suddenly clear. It was Chelsea. The screaming was coming from somewhere behind me and off to the side, but I didn't have time to go figure out where she was. I stopped and looked around—marking

in my head my location, and where her cries were coming from so I could try to go get her if I could later.

I felt horrible for not going to try to save her right then, but what would I do when I got there? I didn't know the codes to enter buildings, and I'm sure her cell was heavily protected. Gareth knew that there were people who liked helping Chelsea—who would do things for her—so he probably had some of his best and most trusted henchman stationed near her quarters.

As I continued moving forward, the trees around me started to become thicker and taller and they were closing in above my head, blocking out the sunlight. I knew I was heading the right way.

I ran up the path, remembering each fork and which way to head. I was confident I was heading in the right direction and I was pleased to see that I wasn't winded and that I could likely outrun anyone else if I had to. But I couldn't outrun a bullet, so the safest thing would be to escape detection.

I wondered what was happening back at the dining hall. Delphine had surely noticed by now that I was missing if she hadn't seen me escape in the moment.

I finally got to the clearing, which was at the bottom of a small mountain where the security cabin was situated at the top. From this distance, I could see Jacob standing just outside, peering down at me. He had his hand up to his forehead, as if to block the sun.

He was silent and stood dead-still as I huffed and puffed up to the peak of the mountain, quickly, collapsing at his feet when I got to the top. That run was on par with our most difficult workout, and by the end of the run, I finally felt gassed.

"Took you long enough," Jacob said, and I couldn't tell if he was being sarcastic or serious. "No time to wait, anyway, get up and come inside," he ordered, offering me one of his hands and helping to lift me up. His skin was cool to the touch.

We went inside to the room with all of the monitors. In the center, I immediately saw Don on the floor with a knife protruding from his stomach. He was dead and I could tell it had happened recently.

"What's going on there?"

"Yes, well, I need your help moving him. Let's get him outside first."

"What happened?"

"He was about to call Gareth to share that he had his suspicions about me, so I had to take care of him—immediately. I couldn't wait. Honestly, I would've rather you take care of it. It was disgusting. But anyway, help me get him out of here."

He lifted Don's arms up and I grabbed his legs. We struggled together to pull his body outside and drag it around to the back of the cabin.

"You're going to have to bury him or Gareth will figure this out," I said.

"Gareth's going to figure everything out soon enough regardless. The days of trying to hide what we're doing are over," Jacob responded.

"Okay. What does that mean?"

"It means that the war starts today."

"But what about the kill switch?" I asked. Jacob looked at me, amused.

"That doesn't actually work. Bertram helped to create it and he had a way to turn it off—which he did before he died. Gareth just thinks he can blow this whole place up, but that's not actually true. It will be funny to see him try if it gets to that point, though. Personally, I've never thought that Gareth would actually use that as an out. He's an extremely proud man who has spent the second half of his life building this place to mirror his demented imagination. For him, it's a Utopia that he's earned—that he's built from the ground up. He's not going to just blow it out of the water. That's an empty threat—trust me."

I didn't feel like I had a choice but to trust Jacob and everything that he said. He was a stranger to me, but we were in this together. We were now connected to each other until we either died or left this place—and both of us depended on the other one telling the truth.

CHAPTER 22

"Now, come on inside already," Jacob said impatiently, as he led me back indoors where all the screens were lit up with images from around the island.

I spotted one screen immediately, of Chelsea in her cell. It looked like an animal's cage, completely exposed to the elements in the front. There was a small sink and toilet, and what appeared to be a simple cot, but that was it. It definitely was even worse than my cell, which was downright luxurious in comparison.

She was wearing just a short nightshirt, and she had a blanket wrapped around herself, like she had a chill even though it was hot outside.

I wondered if she was ill. Her hair was uncombed and I saw her screaming, again and again, as she banged her arms against the cell's bars. I then noticed the bleeding—blood dripping from her hands down her arms. There was a tray of untouched food next to her bed.

"How long has she been doing that?" I asked, worried for her.

Jacob shook his head like he didn't understand me, but said, "Probably on and off like that for days. They've reassigned different Suits to watch her—people that won't fall for her flirtatious advances."

"We need to help her," I said, and I realized how silly I sounded, given that we had other more pressing worries at the moment. She was a beautiful girl, that was for sure, but I didn't think she was given a fair shot in life to experience anything normal—to be a typical teenager. I wanted her to experience that.

"We will see if that's possible. Anyway, we don't

have much time. The Praeclarus members are set to arrive earlier than we had hoped and Gareth will figure out what's happening in the dining hall soon enough. Ames and the team can't hold them back for much longer without setting off alarms."

"Okay, so can we call him now?"

"Yes, let's try again. It's nighttime in Oregon right now," Jacob said, and I felt a surge of adrenaline, certain that my dad would not be working and would pick up the phone.

We walked over to the computer on the far wall and Jacob booted it up again. He pressed several buttons and I heard a dial tone. I swallowed, catching my breath and trying to settle my heart from beating out of my chest.

Jacob pushed me toward the screen and I punched in my dad's number ever so carefully, making sure I didn't misdial by accident. It started to ring. Once. Twice. Three times and my heart sank. What was going on? Why wasn't he answering? If it was the middle of the night, he'd definitely pick up, likely thinking something was wrong with one of his parents or his brother or sister.

"Uhhh . . . hello?" a voice suddenly picked up, filling the whole room.

"Dad! It's me—" I said, and I started crying immediately, feeling completely overwhelmed. I was trying to catch my breath and speak normally so he could understand me.

It was silent for a long moment, and I glanced at Jacob, who looked worried and motioned for me to say something else. He pushed his hands downward a few times quickly, gesturing for me to calm down.

"It's me, Dad. It's Reed," I managed to sputter, and I caught my breath, feeling terrified all of a sudden.

"Who the hell is this? Is this some sort of cruel joke?" he asked, and I was certain it was him. I knew his voice well, and he knew mine. I just needed him to talk more.

"No . . . Dad . . . it's Reed . . . I'm alive. Our boat didn't capsize."

I suddenly heard a shriek on the line and someone yelling beside him, and I could tell it was my mom. She grabbed the phone from him.

"Reed?!" she cried out.

"Yes, Mom, it's me—" I barely managed to get the words out.

"Oh my God. Oh, God. You're alive? Alive! I knew it, somehow—" she said, her words running together. "I don't understand. What happened? Where are you?"

And as I started to talk, my dad suddenly came back on the line. "What do you mean your boat didn't capsize? We saw the wreckage with our eyes. They brought us pictures—the police—"

"Whatever you've seen is a lie, Dad—everything is a lie."

"But they pulled wreckage from the sea," he sputtered, tripping over his own words.

"Well, the boat must've been destroyed after we were taken from it."

Jacob looked impatient, like I needed to get to the meat of the matter. He was glancing at all the screens, watching the activity of everyone on the Island frantically, and he was pacing back and forth behind me, walking fast, like a rat trapped in a cage.

"Who took you? I don't understand! What is happening, Reed? Where are you?"

"Gareth Conway, Dad! It's him!" I cried, wanting to say everything all at once, knowing our time was limited.

"Gareth?" my dad asked. "What are you talking about? I don't understand."

"Gareth Conway faked the boat crash. And he's keeping me and a bunch of other innocent kids on an island."

"What? What are you talking about, Reed? Gareth is dead. He's been dead for nearly twenty years. I'm worried about you, Reed. What's really happening?"

"That's what people think—that Gareth died. But it's all fake. He staged a plane crash, I guess, and built this island in the Indian Ocean."

"What island? I don't understand."

"It's called Praeclarus Island, but we call it Gladiator Island. It's a place for a bunch of rich and powerful men from around the world to come and watch kids fight to the death. They place bets on the fights—"

"What in the—you can't be serious—" my dad muttered, and he became quiet. I could hear him saying something to my mom, and her sobbing loudly in the background.

"Dad—I promise you this is all true, and I need your help," I said. "You have to come get us—there are about one hundred people on the island that are trying to escape."

"One hundred people? That's ludicrous."

"It's the truth—and we are ready to fight back."

"What do you mean?"

"We're ready to stage a war against Gareth and his followers."

"A war?"

"Yes. We will do anything it takes to get out of here, but we're going to need you to give us a way off of the Island—that's been the missing piece—"

"Wait, slow down. Reed. I can't keep up with what you're saying. Just tell me where you are and I can come get you—we'll get the Coast Guard, the police . . . armies . . . whatever it takes to help rescue you."

"No!" I cried out. "It has to be a secret mission. The men and women that come to this island are the people that run the world's armies and will kill all of us if alerted—"

"But then why haven't I heard of this?"

"It's top secret—supposedly the island doesn't even exist on maps."

"Satellite encryption?" my dad asked, doubtful.

"Yes . . . exactly. How did you know?" I asked, confused.

There was a long pause and I heard my dad sigh long and deeply. I could tell my mom was crying in the background.

"What is it, Dad?"

"That is ironic, actually."

"What is?" I asked, not understanding.

"The satellite encryption. I developed that technology thirty-five years ago—sold my patents to Gareth, actually."

"What's his issue with you?"

"That's a very long story, Reed. What else do you know about the Island?" my dad asked, as if he finally fully believed what I was telling him and was trying to figure out how to help.

"That it is in the Indian Ocean—and that it's in a region that's monitored by pirates."

"The Indian Ocean is absolutely gigantic. How big is the Island?"

"I don't know—maybe ten miles long—"

"That's big! Well, how do the visitors get there?"

"By helicopter or by boat."

"And when do they arrive?"

"They come every few weeks—a batch of about thirty to forty people each time. But the next group is set to start arriving in the next couple of days."

"Well, tell me who they are, and I will track them down."

I looked at Jacob and he shook his head no, like it was a bad idea, but I think my dad was right. If he could find those people on their way to the Island—he could follow them.

"You and Mom cannot talk to anyone about this—we will all be killed. Do you understand?"

"Yes, Reed. I trust you."

"And if any of these people get a whiff that you are tracking them, I'll be dead."

"I realize that—"

"You will have to move very, very quickly, Dad.

Everything is about to go down. I'm going to have to fight to survive."

"Okay, do whatever it takes," my dad said. I could hear his voice breaking. Then he added, his voice clear again, "We will be there as soon as we can, Reed. I'll find you, I promise."

And with that, I started sobbing again and I couldn't help myself. "I'm sorry, Dad and I'm sorry, Mom . . . "

"Shh . . . there's no time for that now. You're going to have to fight, Reed. Outsmart Gareth and don't let him have a window to capture you—do you understand? I know you can do it—you've always been so clever—"

"I am going to figure this out. You just need to come find us, and soon. I can't hold off Gareth much longer."

"Okay. Reed—I never thought I'd hear your voice again."

"Me neither, Dad," I managed to croak out through my tears.

"I am so proud of you, Son—of getting through this. I know you are going to do it."

"Me too," I said, but I wasn't so confident. I knew Gareth would be sending all of his forces after me once he got wind that the revolt had started in earnest.

"We love you, Reed, very much—you are going to be okay. You have the power to change your situation," my dad said. Even in this heartfelt conversation, he couldn't help sounding like his same new-age self.

"I know, Dad," I said, and I did believe that.

"Okay, Son, let me get to work—we'll come find you—" he said. There was the sound of shuffling and then my mom came on.

"I love you so much, Reed. I can't believe you're alive—" she said, and started crying again.

And then, just like that, Jacob hung up the phone and turned to me.

"Wait—why'd you hang up?" I asked, angry at him for not letting me say goodbye.

"No time to waste. So, it's done, isn't it? I'm going to do my best to give him some sort of sign where we are. I'm still figuring that out. Do you think he can find us?"

"Yes, I do," I said, but I wasn't sure how quickly he could do it. And if any of the Praeclarus members' staff realized they were being tracked or followed, it would be disastrous.

"So what happens now?" I asked.

"You need to go into hiding, Reed. The dining hall situation will become apparent soon. You can't be out in the open any longer."

"Okay—" I said, nodding my head.

"And if anyone saw that you left the dining hall willingly and weren't forced, they'll tell Gareth, thinking that it benefits them to be loyal, and that they'll get a pass off the Island."

"You mean like Micah did?" I asked, wondering where he was taken.

"Well, except that Micah never left the Island—or at least, not for good."

"Wait . . . what are you talking about? How do you know that?"

"Because I can see nearly everything, Reed, remember?" he said, pointing to all the video screens.

"So what happened to him?" I asked.

"He was taken away in the helicopter, only to have that same helicopter land on the same pad just a few hours later, after you guys were in bed."

"What? Why would they do that? Where did Micah go, then? We haven't seen him."

"Well, interestingly enough, he was taken to the hangar area," Jacob said, raising his eyebrows at me.

"The airplane hangar, with the Creatures?"

"Yes . . . but I haven't seen him since and my cameras only have coverage to the security bank just outside the hangar, so after that, it's really a mystery."

"Do you think he is okay?" I asked. I was

worried for my friend, almost certain that Gareth had had him killed.

"It doesn't look good," Jacob admitted.

What a surprise—another thing that Gareth did to raise false hopes and make people think that he might actually be helping people.

Jacob looked at me carefully and said, "Go further up the mountain, not toward the sea. There are caves in the mountain. When you get to the third cave—the one with a large knotted tree butting up right next to it—there's a large rock blocking the entrance. Move that one, and you'll find a place to hide out. From there, I'll be able to contact you. But I have to go into hiding too. Gareth will be coming for me soon; that is inevitable."

"And what about Ames?" I asked, feeling worried for my friend and adviser.

"Ames is going to have to fend for himself too. It's the only way."

CHAPTER 23

Jacob voiced a command into his wristlet. "All is okay. Feel free to proceed."

He looked up at the screen, where he was watching our dining hall. The men with the machine guns motioned to each other to leave, and like that, they were out the door.

All of the kids who had been facedown on the ground—for probably at least an hour now—got up and started looking around, confused. I noticed Delphine immediately—she stood and she stared at the spot where I had been laying and made an angry face.

She said something to the kids standing next

to her, and everyone turned around, seeming perplexed.

Then, clear as day, I saw her look up at the camera. She gazed directly into it, like she was staring at us. I felt a chill go up my spine. I didn't understand why, but it felt menacing.

Jacob looked at me. "Did you see that?"

"Yes," I said, uneasy. And then I remembered our kiss and how familiar it was and amazing, and I felt bad for having conflicted feelings.

"She's a strange one, isn't she?"

"I don't know what to think about her, honestly," I responded, trying to shake off the feeling I had when she stared directly at the camera, like she knew we were watching.

"So, this is when we separate," Jacob said, handing me a backpack.

"What is this?" I asked.

"A few emergency supplies, to use if necessary. But only if necessary. You got me?"

I nodded. "Where are you going to go?"

"I can't tell you—"

"You can't tell me or you won't?"

"I won't."

"Why not?"

"I've learned to only share what is absolutely necessary. You never know when someone will turn around here."

"Couldn't I say the same about you?"

"Yes, you could, that is true," he said, looking me straight in the eye with his cool stare. "Now get out of here."

He led me to the door and he pushed me out. It was a bright sunny day, and from that vantage point halfway up the mountain, I saw the valley below and then a thick tall forest just past that. It was a beautiful place and I wondered what would happen to the Island after we all left.

Maybe the vegetation would start to overtake the buildings, covering them with moss and leaves, and the grass would grow tall and blanket everything, returning the Island to its natural state. It was a satisfying thought—the Island being over-run by its first inhabitants, the vegetation that had made it so lush. It seemed like a just end to this place. I hoped that Jacob's gut was right and that Gareth wouldn't actually blow it out of the water if his back was up against a wall.

I looked up the mountain, which rose high above me, stretching up into the sky like a green hand. There was no visible path and I realized quickly I'd need to make my own way and find the caves in the thick vegetation.

I opened the backpack and I saw there were bin-oculars, a small hatchet, and a few other wrapped packages.

Suddenly, I heard loud sirens in the distance. *What was that about? It couldn't be good.*

Entering the brush, I pushed away the thick branches and vines that obstructed the path. The branches snapped back and hit me in the face as I moved forward, but I ran upwards as quickly as I could, ignoring the pain as my face was cut with each scrape of the prickly wood.

It was darker up here and a little colder, and it felt like the air was thinner, making it more difficult to breathe.

How would I know when my dad had reached us, or if he had reached us at all? I hoped Jacob was prepared to reach me and that I wasn't just hiding somewhere with no connection to the outside world.

I kept on going, not knowing what I would do if I turned back—where would I go? I could still hear the sirens, but they were getting more and more distant.

Finally I passed a rocky area and saw one cave— that was number one, I was sure of it. I kept on going, feeling confident that there was no one else up here. I was above Gareth's domain—in the area of land that had remained untouched by him. I passed a second, smaller cave, and finally after running up about five more minutes, with blood dripping down my face and my arms and my legs, I finally reached a clearing with a large stone formation. I spotted a gnarled tree right next to a big stone wall. There was a rock blocking it, but not totally—there was a small slit I could slip through.

I wasn't eager to be trapped in there quite yet, feeling safe out in the moment just now, so I turned and looked down. I was amazed by what I saw. It was the whole island, spread out before me. I could look down at everything.

The Coliseum was just a small, little thumbprint. I could also see the hotel area where the Praeclarus members stayed, our living quarters, and the hangar. From this vantage point, I thought I could spot a piece of land pushing past the hangar—like a point. I couldn't tell for sure, but I was surprised that there was indeed land even further out, just like Ames and Jacob had suspected. The Island was even bigger than I had realized.

Maybe there was an airstrip back there. I thought about my dad, about him coming to help us, and his words about outsmarting Gareth and being strong enough.

It felt good that he actually believed in me, something I hadn't experienced for so long. I wanted to get back home and prove to him that I was worthy of his faith in me. I was going to do big things—I felt for the first time that it was indeed true, that I could be successful if given the chance.

I had done it here—I had defied the odds, I had sobered up, I faced things that I had never imagined possible, and I had grown tougher, yet also darker. Being away from hurting and killing people—as it had been a few weeks since the last battle—I realized I had started to feel normal again, and hopeful. The darkness was leaving me, exiting my body with every day that passed. It was good to be up against the brink, and now I was becoming Reed again—the person I knew before my brother died.

I took one last look at the outside and turned to face the cave entrance. *It's now or never*, I thought, and I walked up to the opening and slid through the door.

"Hello, stranger," a voice called out, and the person held up a lantern, illuminating the space. It was Chelsea. I couldn't believe my eyes. How did she get here—I had just seen the video of her in her cell.

The room was dim, but I saw that she was cut up and that her face had scratches all over it. Blood dripped from her hands. She looked exhausted, but still beautiful.

"What happened to you? And how did you get here?"

"It was a gift from Jacob. He let me out while the men who were watching my cell were gone. He told me to head up here and that you'd be here with me."

"Are you okay?" I asked and went over and stared at her more closely. She set the lantern on a small table, and I looked around and realized this was a full room—with a bed, a small bookshelf, a table, and another small bench to sit on.

"What is this place?" I asked, confused that it was furnished.

"It's my secret hiding spot, where Odin and I used to come when we wanted to be alone. It was the only way we could be together."

"How did you guys get furniture up here?" It seemed impossible through such a forested area with no path.

"Elise did it for us. I'm not sure how, honestly, but I think Odin's dad helped as well."

"About Elise—"

"She's dead, isn't she?" Chelsea asked and her eyes filled with tears. "Everyone I've ever cared for has been killed by Gareth. Except you."

"I need to tell you something else about Elise."

She looked at me, biting her lip, and I sat her down on the bed.

"Gareth told us Elise was your mother."

"What? I don't understand. My mother died

when I was very young. Elise took care of her when she died."

"That's just what they told you."

Chelsea looked devastated, but she didn't cry at all and I saw anger set in her eyes and jaw.

"Why would they do that? And why wouldn't Elise tell me the truth? It doesn't make sense."

"I don't know—they had a falling out—maybe Gareth didn't want you to side with her? Maybe he forbade her telling you the truth?"

"She tried to help me—she helped me and Odin be together," she said, and a single tear rolled down the side of her cheek. "It was like she did what she could to help me be happy—to have even just a sliver of normalcy here."

"That must've been hard for her to not tell you the truth. She wanted to escape, and we were going to bring you with us. I think that was her ultimate plan." I reached over and hugged her close to me, and she was still for a long time.

There were no other sounds except our

breathing, and I felt like this was what made sense, us being together.

"I want to talk to you about something," I finally said, and she pulled back and looked at me, her big eyes serious but determined.

"What is it?"

"If we get out of here, I want you to come to Oregon with me. Come live there with us, with my family."

"Really?" she asked, and I felt her whole body collapse into me. "I don't understand, Reed. Why don't you hate me? It's not just because you think I'm pretty?"

"No, that's not it, although you are a beautiful girl."

She smiled ever so slightly.

"I think we grew up in parallel paths, with famous fathers that are larger than life. I took my dad for granted, and all the things I had in my life—I took all that for granted too. Seeing how you were raised and what you've been subjected to, I want to show you that there's a whole bigger, better world out there and that you can be a part of it. I think you deserve it."

"You're so nice to me, when I was cruel to you."

"I'm forgiving you. And if we're going to make it out of here, we need to work together."

"Okay."

"Okay?"

"Yes, okay. I will come to Oregon with you," she said and then grew quiet, like she was deep in thought.

She finally spoke again, "But what about your parents? They're not going to want some weird other kid around."

"You'd be surprised. I bet they'll welcome it. My parents are kind people, even if we didn't always see eye-to-eye. They mean well and I think if I say that you're okay, they'll agree."

"Okay. So, what is the plan?"

"I contacted my dad. He knows that I'm alive and out in the world somewhere. He just needs to figure out how to find us, and he'll provide the helicopters and boats to get us out of here."

"But Gareth will know that we've gone missing as soon as someone tips him off that Ames and crew ambushed the dining hall and that you escaped."

"I know, that's why we have to hide and wait."

"And what about Delphine and Micah?" she asked. "Aren't they your best friends? Where are they?"

I shook my head, uncertain where they both were. I remembered Delphine's stare and then her kiss, and felt bad for being uneasy about her at all. She was down there and Micah was in the hangar, or more likely dead. What could I do to help them from so far away?

CHAPTER 24

"I don't know. Jacob said that Micah got taken to the hangar, which doesn't make sense, and something about Delphine has been off."

"What do you mean?" she asked me, looking concerned.

"She just seems to be acting shiftier, I guess. I don't know. I can't really put my finger on it," I said.

"Hmph," Chelsea said, her face looking dark in thought. "Micah was taken to the hangar? That's odd," Chelsea said, and we both sat quietly, thinking. "That's where the Creatures are held. Why would he be brought there?"

"I think he might be dead—maybe Gareth

sacrificed him to the Creatures. And did you know that just past the hangar there's more land?"

"Yes, I knew there was more land past there, but I've never been able to reach it. It's protected by tall rock walls and barbed wire."

"Well, I saw it with my binoculars when I came up here—you want to see it too? Maybe you can figure out what's going on over there."

She looked at me with raised eyebrows. "Can we go out there? Is it safe?"

"No one else is coming up here. It's a secret place, isn't it?"

"Yes, of course," she said, and I took her hand and we squeezed out of the opening in the cave.

We stood on the top of the hill, looking down at the Island.

"It is quite beautiful, isn't it?" she asked me. "I used to just stand up here and stare out at the land and the ocean and dream of what existed outside of this place—"

"I don't blame you. There's a lot more than what you've seen here. A lot more good."

"I hope you are right."

"So, look. Here—" I handed her the binoculars and pointed toward the giant structure. "Take a look and you'll see there's something beyond the hangar. I think there are buildings over there."

She put the binoculars up to her eyes and squinted, gazing through them for a long time.

"What is that?" Chelsea asked.

"I know, right? There are buildings over there," I said.

"No, check this out," Chelsea said, looking worried as she handed the binoculars to me. "Something is happening at the hangar."

I put the instrument up to my face and looked through, staring down at the structure. Chelsea was right; something was amiss. I saw that a corner of the building was on fire—they were just small flames at first but were becoming bigger and bigger—the flames reaching up into the sky. A column of thick, black smoke filled the sky.

"What's happening?" she asked, and now the fire was easy to see, even without the binoculars.

I strained to make sense of the scene. I thought I saw people running out of the hangar doors—many people, some looked like kids. They were spilling out of the building and running away from it toward the other side of the Island.

I brought my attention back toward the hangar, its left side now almost fully engulfed in flames. I couldn't believe my eyes. What was happening?

Then, as I stared down at the building, I spotted animals starting to run out, away from the smoke that was undoubtedly filling the building. Someone must've let the Creatures out and they were fleeing from the fire as well. I wondered if Gareth had prepared for a fire, or if he had started it himself to create more chaos.

Chelsea turned to me, wide-eyed, "What do we do?"

"We stay here for now, and wait to see what happens."

I thought of Micah. Was there any chance he was still alive? I scanned the crowd of people fleeing, hoping to see him mixed in, but he wasn't there. Was he okay? I had a pang of guilt about being up here, safe, while my friends were still back in the training area. What would happen to them when they heard about the fire? Would Gareth do something?

I opened my bag and I found a wristlet with Jacob's info programmed into it.

I connected to him, and his face popped up on the screen.

"Where are you?" I asked. As his picture went in and out, I saw that he was surrounded by smoke.

"I did it . . . I . . . started . . . this . . . " he yelled, as he was engulfed in gray smoke. I couldn't even see his face now.

He was choking and coughing.

"What did you do?"

"I started the fire . . . to try to stop the Praeclarus members from coming. The smoke cloud will be huge. They will turn around if they see the Island is in flames," he sputtered. "But, I have to go now . . . I need to get . . . out . . . of here . . . " he called out, and then he disconnected, the screen went dark.

"We can't stay up here," I said.

"What do you mean? We can't go down there," she said, looking at me with a worried grimace. "It's chaos."

I thought of my friends on the other side of the Island caught in the cross-fire of the revolt. What would Gareth do to them? I imagined Delphine being taken hostage, ordering his Suits to kill the rest, or worse. "I have to do something to help them. I couldn't live with myself if they were killed while I just sat up here, waiting for rescue."

"Are you sure?" she asked me, seeming doubtful.

"Yes."

"Okay, then I'm going with you," Chelsea said, and she held on to my arm.

I had no idea what we were running toward as we grabbed hands and started to jog down the mountain. She was a little bit slower than me—having not been in grueling physical training every day for months—but she was a good sport, silent, and determined as we headed into God knew what.

We got into the valley and were about to head into the thickly forested area, when she turned toward me.

"Whatever happens, you'll stick with me, right?" she asked, her face set in worry.

"Of course . . . we're in this together, okay?" I asked, and I hugged her quickly. We didn't have time to wait or even pretend to be romantic. If things were on fire, I had to go help everyone.

As we ran into the woods and turned a corner, all of a sudden another person came up the path.

It was Delphine. But it wasn't. It was like looking at Delphine, but younger. Like I was seeing

Delphine in reverse. Like a fourteen-year-old version of her.

My brain didn't keep up with what was happening and I looked over at Chelsea, confused.

Chelsea seemed scared.

The person who looked like Delphine appeared terrified too. She made a weird snarled sound at us and raised up her arms, like she was going to attack us.

But I had the hatchet in my hand, and there wasn't much she could do to hurt us, if she wanted to.

"Delphine?" I asked, and the girl lowered her arms and looked surprised.

"Delphine? You think I'm Delphine?" Her voice was completely different, with a strong accent—not American. She started laughing like it was the most hilarious thing ever.

"I wish I was Delphine—the golden child. Delphine gets everything, doesn't she? And who are you, anyway?"

"Wait . . . who are you?" Chelsea called out. It didn't compute.

This person looked exactly like Delphine. The same crazy red hair. The weird, green sparkling eyes and pixie face. I didn't see anything different—at all—aside from her being smaller and younger.

"I'm Duae," she explained. "The second. The same, but not quite. Two years younger, and a whole lot less lucky."

"What do you mean?" I asked.

"Well, I'm not Delphine. Gareth's made that clear."

"Gareth? What does he have to do with this?"

"Gareth's my maker, of course," she said, and smiled as she walked closer to us. I had my guard up, just in case she was about to attack.

"Your maker? Like your dad?" I asked.

"No, not my dad. My creator."

It didn't make sense at all what we were looking at until suddenly it dawned on me. It reminded me of the sci-fi movies I liked to watch when I was stoned.

"You mean—you're like a clone?"

Chelsea looked over at me, confused. "A what?"

"A clone. A scientific imprint of Delphine." I turned to the girl. "You're the same, genetically, aren't you?"

The strange girl smiled and stared at me with those familiar, twinkly eyes. "Well, that's not what we're called, but that's how it's explained. We're like, his soldiers. Gareth is making us into an army."

I was frightened by this bizarre turn of events, another instance of Gareth being more dangerous than I could've ever imagined. All I could think about was Delphine. I was absolutely sick to my stomach all of a sudden. My head hurt and I felt like I needed to sit down. Chelsea was squeezing my arm, hard, her fingernails digging into my skin.

I had to get it together. My dad was on his way. *What did this all mean?*

"How many of you are there?" I finally asked.

"Wouldn't you like to know?"

"So, where were you running to, just now? Trying to get away?" I asked and the girl looked embarrassed, like I caught her in a lie.

"Where are you going? Trying to get killed?" she responded quickly, smirking at me.

"What do you mean?"

"It's a mess. I'd think twice before running down there."

I did think twice, about Delphine especially. I was terrified and furious. Everything she'd done was a lie. It was clear now. I'm not sure how she got away with it, but it was true.

Ship Out—a lie. Our friendship—a total lie. Why and how did she do it?

So, was she was just one of Gareth's army? I was amazed how she had faked everything so perfectly, had made no mistakes. *Was I the target all along?*

I was filled with a rage toward her and

everything she'd done to trick me. If I could get my hands on her, I'd surely kill her.

"Did you know?" I asked Chelsea, feeling confused about whether or not I could trust anyone at all. It was one lie after another.

"I had no idea, I swear," she said, then turned to Duae. "But, where did you come from? I've been on this island my whole life. How could I have never seen you?"

"Because we lived in the hangar, and in the Triangle."

"The Triangle? What is that?" Chelsea asked.

"Oh. Yes, it's the area just behind the hangar. That small plot of land is all I've ever known. So this—" she said, waving her arm at her surroundings, "this is freedom to me. I'm not going back."

"We can't go down there right now," Chelsea said, and I agreed. I wasn't going to run into a trap. We needed to think this through.

"What if the fire spreads across the Island,"

I said, worried that if it eventually headed up the mountain that would spell certain doom for us.

"Gareth already sent his crew to help contain it—but he was too late—one of the scientists let us all out, and the Creatures. They wanted to make sure we didn't die. So, I have no idea how many of us went rogue," Duae said, shrugging.

In the distance, the large black cloud billowed up into the sky and spread out like a toxic mushroom.

If my dad was coming, I guessed he could see the cloud in real-time satellite data, but there'd be no landmass underneath it. What was previously just a patch of ocean would now have a mysterious cloud rising above it. It was a clue, and I wondered if that was what Jacob had hinted at trying to do—to give my dad just a tiny hint at our location.

We had to retreat, and I felt we had no choice but to bring Duae with us. If she was telling the truth, then she could be a good ally. And if she was lying, I certainly didn't want her escaping to go tell Gareth where we were hiding.

"Come on, let's go back up and figure out our next steps," I said. Chelsea agreed and Duae followed close behind, acting relieved to have some companionship. She talked non-stop the whole way up the mountain and seemed happy to have someone to chat with. She didn't appear that worried about what was happening down below.

I ignored all her chattering, trying to collect myself and contain the anger and confusion that made it hard to put one foot in front of the other.

When we got to the top, I peered through the binoculars. It looked like the fire was still burning, but there was a group of Suits with long hoses spraying water at it, trying to contain it.

I wondered how many Creatures had escaped and where they were now. I was less scared of the humans on the island, but knew the Creatures were engineered to kill people easily, given their size. I wouldn't want to encounter one by accident on one of the trails.

"Let's go back in the cave," I instructed and we each slid through the small opening and sat down, looking at each other.

I tried to channel my dad's words—that I was strong enough to handle whatever I faced, and that I'd need to use my brain and my wits to get out of this increasingly bizarre and scary situation.

Chelsea reached over and held my hand, squeezing it, which made Duae giggle.

"I've never seen anyone except Delphine and Micah do that," she said.

My stomach dropped. "What do you mean? Delphine and Micah? How do you know Micah?"

Duae laughed even harder, covering her mouth with both hands.

"Oh! Micah? He's also one of us. You know him too?"

"Yes, I know Micah," I said, although that really felt so very far from the truth. *He was a clone as well?* I couldn't believe it and I pressed my hand to my forehead, squeezing it. *What was happening?*

I felt like every single thing I'd learned since being on the boat was in question, and I couldn't help but pull away after Chelsea clenched my hand even harder, looking at me like she was terrified.

The fight ahead was going to be even more treacherous than I could've possibly imagined. The revolt was underway, and I wouldn't have Delphine or Micah by my side, how I'd always imagined. Instead, I knew that to get out of here alive, I'd likely have to kill them.